The T

SPANISH MAIN

TREVOR ANDERSON

First published in paperback by
Michael Terence Publishing in 2024
www.mtp.agency

ISBN 9781800947269

All characters and events in this publication,
other than those in the public domain, are fictitious,
and any resemblance to real persons, is purely coincidental

Michael Terence
Publishing

One

Jack pushed off the small skiff from the beach at Sennac Bay and clambered in, getting one foot wet as he did so. His best friend Tom was at the oars and pulled away from the harbour wall in smooth well-practised strokes. The front of the aluminium boat lifted slightly as the low waves broke underneath them. It was early morning on a beautiful, late July day. The sea was shimmering, calm and clear with the tide just starting to come in.

Jack Andrews and Tom Williams, both aged twelve, almost thirteen, were inseparable; they spent all their available time together. It was the beginning of the summer holidays and a glorious six weeks stretched ahead of them. They lived in the village of Sennac, on the north coast of the county of Cornwall, in south west England. Jack and Tom had met and played together from the age of five after meeting on their first day at school. They were tall for their age, both slim and athletic; they loved sports and were extremely competitive.

Tom was as dark as Jack was fair. Both accomplished swimmers and sailors who always wore lifejackets when in a boat, their parents didn't mind them staying inside the calm waters of the horseshoe-shaped Mennan Cove in their small skiff, an aluminium rowing boat. This was a small bay about four hundred yards across at its widest point, with a harbour wall on one side where the small fishing boats and pleasure craft were moored. On the other side, were low cliffs which had a cave worn away into the rock by the relentless sea. A frequent pastime for them was to spend a few hours fishing and snorkelling with the skiff tied to an old mooring post on fine, calm days. Tom was already headed for their favourite spot using his best economical oar action. The deal was that Tom rowed the short distance there and Jack rowed back.

Local legend had it that the cove had been a landing point for smugglers for around two hundred years from the 17th to 19th centuries. Jack and Tom reckoned that there must have been something in the story because there were steps cut into the rocky cliffs and an ancient mooring post at the bottom. They would have loved to have retraced the route of pirates and smugglers; and had climbed up numerous times but the steps ended below the top of the cliff where there had been a rock fall.

As they got closer to the cliff, Mennan cave loomed to their left and the steps and mooring post, where they tied up the skiff, to their right. Their parents strictly forbade them to go into the cave because the water reached the cave's ceiling at high tide. The temptation had always been there but they had resisted.

"Come on Tom! Put your back into it!" roared Jack, "head for the steps."

Irritated by what he though an unnecessary remark, Tom responded, "Oh shut up, you idiot! I am, but we're being pulled to the left, it feels like the current is running that way!"

Jack could see that they were indeed heading in the direction of the cave and a slight shiver went through him. He wasn't sure if it was fear or excitement.

"Here, let me take one of the oars," Jack said, as he wedged himself onto the seat next to Tom. They pulled together but to no avail. Their boat was being drawn as if by an invisible rope towards the cave. In a matter of minutes they were just twenty yards from the entrance. They rowed harder and faster.

"Yes! We're making some headway," yelled Tom, turning around to check their direction.

Their efforts appeared to be working; the bow of the skiff was edging away from the mouth of the cave. They were definitely heading towards the steps but they were breathless with the effort, their lungs on fire and arms started to weaken as they drained of strength. Still rowing, but slower now, they felt relieved that they were making progress in the right direction. Suddenly without warning they were turned sharply to the left and they were carried along faster, which made them work even harder but to no avail. They were heading straight for the cave.

"What are we going to do?" cried Tom, "let's jump out and swim for it!"

"No! We'll just get carried along by this current, let's just see what happens, we're safer in the boat."

They looked around, there was no one to be seen in a boat or walking on the harbour wall, it was pointless to yell for help. The boys only ever took one mobile phone with them on fishing trips, this time it was Tom who had his, tucked away in a waterproof bag inside his pack. He desperately tried to get it out, but they were all too quickly at the mouth of the cave, with darkness looming. Having got it, he looked at it. No signal; they were helpless.

The skiff was soon at the mouth of the cave, darkness looming, Jack and Tom had stopped rowing, shipped the oars and waited ominously, expecting something awful. The current carried them into the cave, into the dark. Within moments the daylight behind them was receding and they couldn't see anything, the only sensation now was the sound of the water lapping on their boat and on the sides of the cave. They continued in silence for what seemed an age but was probably only ten minutes till Tom suddenly spoke in almost a whisper.

"Jack, does it seem warmer to you?"

"I was just going to ask you the same," responded Jack. "It feels like when we got out of the airport when we went to Florida two years ago."

The air in the cave had taken on unusual warmth, humid air enveloped them. Both boys were silent, fear coursed through their bodies; just the lap of the water on the rocks broke the silence. They seemed to lose all sensation of time. They had no idea of how much time had passed as Jack hadn't even thought to look at his digital watch, which lit up at the touch of a button.

Jack cried out, "Tom! I think I can see some light ahead!"

"Yes, you're right, definitely!" replied Tom, somewhat relieved.

The walls of the cave were now just visible, the nooks and crannies were in shadow where the light hit the raised outcrops as it became brighter by the moment. The water had a strange translucence, they could see fish just below the surface, it was so clear to a great depth. Ahead, the opening of the cave was getting closer.

"Look at the sea Tom!" Jack exclaimed, "it's an amazing colour!"

The sea was turquoise and lit by a bright hot sun. The boat exited the cave and they had to shield their eyes from the glare. The heat was oppressive with high humidity.

"What's going on Jack? Where are we and why is it so hot and… and, err… different?"

They looked around in awe. The clifftops behind them were covered in tropical growth, with palm trees swaying in the breeze. Large birds sailed effortlessly across the deep blue sky.

"Looks like we're in another country, but how?"

"I really don't know Jack, but I think we've got company!"

Jack glanced around to look in the same direction as Tom. To their left was a rocky promontory that stuck out from the cliff. Sailing into view was the most amazing sight. Rounding the point and proceeding in full sail across their bow, not one hundred yards ahead of them was a galleon, which looked like something out of a "Pirates of the Caribbean" film.

They could make out the name, painted on the bow, "The Pelican". Men on deck were shouting and pointing at the boys. Jack and Tom could hear orders being called out.

"Heave to! Weigh anchor!"

Jack, almost in wonder, said, "They must be making a film."

"Maybe, but what are we doing in what appears to be a hot foreign country? This makes no sense."

Both boys had confused, awe-stricken looks on their faces. They watched as the crew hauled on ropes pulling up the sails. The anchor chain could be heard screeching and clanking as the anchor found its way to the sea bottom. Over the next few minutes, the ship turned slightly to the right of its original direction as it stopped, anchored up and a longboat was quickly launched down the side with nine men aboard. A large man with a beard and long hair leant over the ships rail and pointed at Jack and Tom then shouted orders to the crew in the rowing boat. His instructions frightened the boys to their very core.

"Catch 'em and bring 'em 'ere!"

"Tom, I'm not sure this is a film. Err… are you thinking what I'm thinking?"

"Yes I am! Let's get out of here!"

They quickly shrugged off their life jackets, took to the oars and started rowing back towards the cave but made no headway, it was as if they were rowing against the tide.

"No good," yelled Tom, "quick, head for the beach!"

They turned and made towards a beach they could see in an inlet about two hundred yards away. They were being chased; the large rowing boat from the galleon was some distance behind, but gaining on them. With eight men at the oars and one at the tiller, the crew were all burly men obviously used to strenuous exercise. Facing the rear as they rowed, the boys were looking straight at their pursuers and could see that they were scruffy and rough-looking specimens.

"I don't want anything to do with those guys Tom, I think they're pirates!" panted Jack.

"I think you're right, keep going, harder!"

Jack and Tom, lungs on fire, sweating from the heat and the effort, were rowing as fast as they could. The beach, the small golden patch of sand they were heading for, in their distress, looked just as far as when they had started rowing, they seemed to be making little headway. Fearing for their lives, they kept the rapid rowing action going and after what seemed an eternity, they were gradually approaching the beach where small breakers were lifting their skiff and carrying them forward. The pursuing boat was less than fifty yards behind. Suddenly, the boys felt the skiff hit sand in the shallows and grind a halt. They leapt out and started running up the beach as fast as their legs could carry them towards cover, just leaving their boat in the shallows. Looking back around, Jack and Tom saw that the pursuers had beached and were jumping out of their longboat. They were carrying what looked like muskets and swords! The boys reached the cover of the trees and panting for breath, they slowed to a trot through the dense undergrowth. All manner of creatures were chattering and screeching, it reminded Jack of a nature programme on TV. The ground began to slope steeply upwards and climbing was difficult because it was slippery. Tom looked back and saw they were leaving tracks. The sole patterns of their shoes were evident with every step. He said in a half whisper, "Jack, we've got to get onto harder ground like rocks or something. We're leaving a trail they can follow."

Jack glanced down and agreed immediately.

"OK! Where do we go though?"

They could hear crashing and shouting below them, terrifyingly, quite close by the sound of things. Forgetting the issue of leaving a trail, they started to hurry again and it was tough going. Just when they thought their legs would carry them no further they burst into a clearing. A hundred yards or so ahead of them was a rock face, almost vertical, craggy and formidable-looking, but it was their only route. Running as hard as they could, reaching the wall of rock, the boys started their accent, pulling themselves hand over hand as quickly as they could. The rocks were dry and hot from the sun; small lizards scurried into cracks and crevices, darting away from the boys. Having reached a good height above the clearing below, the boys looked down. The pirates were just starting their climb, but four of them with long muskets were kneeling down and aiming up towards Jack and Tom.

"Quick!" cried out Jack, "keep going. Over to the left, there's a huge rock sticking out we might be able to get behind it!"

Crack! crack! crack! crack! The muskets fired almost simultaneously. Musket balls smacked into the rocks above the boys, and stone chips rained down. The shouting from below was incessant; they were like baying hounds after a fox.

"Stop! or we'll shoot 'ee!"

"Keep going," yelled Jack. "I don't think they want to shoot us. I think they're trying to scare us!"

"Well they've succeeded," said Tom. "I'm terrified!"

Moving laterally along a ledge, they made the outcrop of rock and got behind it, now out of sight of the pirates. Ahead was a climb of about another hundred feet to get to what appeared to be the top.

"Come on, if we can get over the top we might be able to find a place to hide."

Jack wasn't going to argue, tired and terrified, he was as desperate as Tom to get away from these guys. Scrambling and pulling themselves higher and higher, occasionally having to give each other a hand, they made steady progress. With a supreme final burst of energy and effort, they got to the summit. Looking back they saw the first pirates coming around the rocky outcrop. The pirates saw them and started yelling again. Jack and Tom didn't hang around to hear what they were shouting but could guess. Looking ahead, across a bare, almost level rocky plateau several hundred yards wide was another almost vertical cliff face.

"Oh my goodness!" exclaimed Tom. "What do we do now?"

"We keep going, that's what we do."

They dashed across the open ground, legs tiring but terror and adrenalin keeping them moving. The pirates had reached the plateau. More shots were being fired; musket balls ricocheted to the left and right of Jack and Tom. Within a few minutes they reached the cliff face and stopped. Looking behind, the pirates were half way across the ground between them. They had moments to make a decision, climb or give up.

"What now Jack?" cried Tom. "We run this way, follow me!"

Jack had spotted something and set off to their left, running along the base of the cliff with Tom close behind. This made the pirates change direction, angling towards the boys, two hundred yards behind.

"In here, quick!" yelled Jack. It was a cave. Two caves in one day, thought Jack. It's crazy!

They dashed into what was a huge opening with a yawning blackness in front of them and ran until the daylight behind them was lost. Shuffling forward in the dark, their eyes struggling to adjust to the lack of light, they were moving very slowly, hearts pounding with fear.

"Stay close," whispered Tom, "it would be stupid to lose each other."

At that, they heard crashing footsteps and shouting. The pirates had entered the cave.

"They won't be able to see us," said Jack. "Let's keep going."

They made their way slowly in the dark, edging forward, occasionally stumbling on loose rocks, and banging their knees on protruding boulders. The sides of the cave were getting narrower. With their hands in front of them they felt their way around a sharp bend.

"Tom! It's getting lighter," whispered Jack.

"Yes!" Relief flooded through them both.

Although still gloomy, they had enough light to see ahead that there was an area of the cave becoming visible to them. Their spirits leapt and they picked up the pace and headed towards the light and were now able to see where they put their feet, they hurried on. Soon they entered a huge chamber that was riven out of the natural rock probably millions of years ago. Sunlight streamed down through an opening high above them.

"We've got to get up there, it's the way out."

"OK, let's look for a way up," responded Tom.

The momentary silence while the boys looked around the cavern was shattered by voices, too close for comfort.

"They're here! Quick Jack, we might be able to hide in that niche in the rock over there."

Tom led the way to the other side of the cavern and a fissure, about as wide as their bodies, became evident. Tom slid in and soon was lost to sight from Jack, who was following quickly behind. The opening went back about twenty feet and the boys got in as far as they could. They squeezed down onto their bottoms facing the way they had come. It was pitch dark. They couldn't see the cavernous chamber so they couldn't be seen, tucked away in the rocky cleft. They sat quietly, breathing as slowly and quietly as they could. The pirates entered the chamber, cursing and swearing.

"Where 'ave the little devils gone?" groaned one of the gang. "Reckon they've climbed out up there," he said pointing up to the opening.

"The Cap'ns goin' to be furious with us, losing two boys. 'ee fancied 'em for a ransom, 'ee did."

The man doing most of the talking appeared to be in charge. He was bigger than all the rest, had a patch over one eye and a long scar down his right cheek, beard stubble covered his jaw.

"What shall we do then Ned?" asked a burly guy with a red bandana tied on his head.

"Well, Albert, we look around this cavern first."

Jabbing his finger at four of the group he said, "You lot look over that side and make sure you do a proper job. The rest of you spread out over this side."

They began a search, looking behind boulders, up the rock face and anywhere they thought the boys might hide. Ned came to the fissure the boys were hiding in.

"Jasper, get over 'ere!" he called out.

The youngest of the group, a slim and lithe-looking boy of about fifteen or sixteen came forward.

"Yes Ned."

"Get into that there crack in the rock me lad and see if they are in there."

Jasper went in and was soon approaching where the boys were. On hearing Ned's orders and Jasper's slow crunching footsteps towards them, Jack and Tom froze in terror. Their nerves were jangling. As it got narrower towards the end, Jasper was feeling his way in the dark. He dropped to his knees and put out his hand. He touched Jack, gripping his arm. He quickly dropped his hand and shuffled backwards on his knees.

Jack thought, "This is it. The game is up!" He was trembling with fear.

Jasper got to his feet and edged backwards out of the fissure.

"No, not in there Ned," he called out.

Both boys heaved a very silent but large sigh of relief.

"Let's climb out of 'ere me hearties. Maybe they're outside waitin' for us, eh?" Ned laughed at his own joke.

At that, the pirates started the perilous climb out of the cavern. They made their way hanging onto rocky outcrops and hauling themselves up, with boots slipping and sliding, cursing all the way. Eventually, they made it out and after a cursory search, looking for footprints or likely hiding places; they began their descent to the longboat.

In the cavern, the boys waited for a half an hour, not moving or talking to be sure the pirates had gone. When they were certain they couldn't hear anything, they crawled out of their hiding place.

Jack in a loud whisper said, with a good deal of emotion is his voice.

"They want to kidnap us and hold us for a ransom!"

"I heard," retorted Tom. "Let's not get caught then. Come on, they climbed out, we can do it too!"

"Wait!" said Jack, "they're up here looking for us, let's go back the way we came, we might be able to get our skiff."

"I don't think so. I don't want to have to climb down that cliff face and they may have left someone guarding our boat. I think we climb out and hope they've gone off looking for us."

"Okay," Jack saw the sense in that.

The boys made their way gingerly up the sloping rock face towards the opening. Slowly but surely, they got to the top without mishap. Peering out without standing, the boys saw that they were high up and had a view of much of the land in front of them. The ground fell away to a wooded slope, which levelled out before the beach. Looking out over the top of the trees and off to the left, they could see four of the pirates standing around where their longboat had been. The boy's skiff had been pulled higher up the beach. Turning their gaze towards the galleon, the rowing boat was now on its way back to the ship crewed by the other five.

"Tom, my mind is in a whirl. What is going on here? We get sucked through Mennan Cave; we come out in a hot country and get chased by pirates, apparently from another century who want to kidnap us for ransom. One of them finds us but he doesn't tell the others. Can you make any sense of this?"

"Maybe we got pulled through a time warp. You know, there are loads of stories about that sort of thing."

"Yes, but who believes them. They're fiction!"

"Well, whatever the case, we are where we are and have to get out of here. We need our boat back."

The boys looked wistfully down at where the pirates had pulled their skiff out of the water. It was beached just up from the waterline.

"I wonder if we can distract those guys and get the boat back. Come on Tom, let's make a plan! Keep low and let's get out of sight till we decide what we are going to do."

They scrambled out and crawled down a few yards to a group of trees where from the shade they could see the four pirates and their skiff. They surveyed the ground in front and below them. A hundred yards to the left of the pirates was a small rocky cliff directly over the sea and the top of which looked about thirty feet or so above the water.

"What do you think of this Tom? We can make our way down there. I'll stay inside the trees and get around behind them, then up onto that bit of cliff to their left and let them see me. They will, I hope, give chase. Meanwhile, you dash from the cover of the trees and launch the skiff. When they are far enough away from both of us, I jump into the sea, swim out and you pick me up. Reckon we could do that?"

"I can't think of anything better than that, Jack. Let's do it!"

"Right then, just so we know what we're doing, let's make our way down through the trees. When we get to the lower ground, I'll go off to the left and get around behind the pirates to the cliff. I'll get up onto it make some noise." Jack paused, "Yeah, I know what I'll do, I'll pretend to fall, cry out and hopefully they will come after me. You keep your eyes on them and when they are half way across towards me, you get the skiff launched. When I see you out on the water I'll jump off the cliff and swim towards you. OK?"

"Okay Jack, I'll do my best."

They started their way down, slowly, carefully, trying not to fall and especially not to make a noise. Once in the trees they lost sight of the pirates. The heat was oppressive and the boys were sweating profusely and very thirsty. They came to a stream tumbling and gurgling down its rocky course. Stopping, they plunged their faces into the cold, refreshing water.

Drinking their fill and cooling off at the same time, it made them feel a bit better.

They were approaching the bottom of the slope and the ground was levelling off. The edge of the trees was just a few yards in front of them now and they could see the sandy beach and the glistening sea just ahead. They kept moving until they were almost directly in line with the pirates and their skiff, about fifty yards away.

Jack whispered in Tom's ear. "Right Tom, you crouch down and wait here and I'll get around through the trees until I am opposite the cliff. When you hear me shouting, make sure the pirates are running towards me then go for it. You okay with that?"

"Yes, but I'm really scared Jack."

"So am I Tom, but it's the only thing I can think of to get us away from here. I'm going, good luck chum."

Jack was away then, moving cautiously again, keeping back in the shadow of trees. He held his breath as he passed the pirates who were now sitting down on a couple of large boulders on the edge of the beach. They couldn't possibly have heard him breathing heavily as they were too far away but he was so nervous and his heart was beating so furiously he was sure they would hear it and turn around. At one point he tripped over some roots and crashed to the ground almost crying out but he managed to keep silent although he banged his knee quite hard. Recovering, Jack set off again and in a few minutes was opposite the cliff perched over the sea. He crept forward to the edge of the trees. He was going to have to make a short dash across open ground to the beginning of the rocky slope which was like a ramp, leading up to the top of the cliff.

Jack looked in the direction of the pirates; they had their backs to him. He stepped out into the open. The full glare of the hot sun hit him as he started to run, pounding over the sand as he made it to the rocky slope and had to slow down as the angle of the rock got steeper. Moving to his left, he moved along a flat ledge, which meant he was able to keep going with only his head and shoulders showing above the top of the outcrop between him and the pirates. Glancing to his right he could see they were still facing away from him.

Moving up to the top of the rock he looked for a suitable place to "fall". The rock was quite flat at this point but he didn't want to overdo it and fall off the thing. Right, he was ready, summoning up his courage, he lay down face first on the rock in what was full view to the pirates and gave an almighty yell.

"Aaaghhh!" And another, "Ouchhhh!"

Along the beach, he saw the pirates stand up and look his way almost in one motion. Jack got up and rubbed his knees as if he had been hurt. He called out to an imaginary Tom below and to his left, pointing and waving for effect. Glancing to his right again he saw that the pirates were running along the beach towards him. Over their shoulders he saw Tom dashing from cover and running towards the skiff. The plan was working!

Jack ran to his left again so only his head and shoulders were showing with the top of the rock between him and the pirates again.

He called out to the imaginary Tom once more.

"Quick! Over this way!"

He didn't know if the pirates could hear what he was saying but he felt they should think at this point that he and Tom were still together. He ran back up onto the top and made it to the edge of the cliff and looked down.

"What am I doing?" Jack exclaimed. It was a long way down to the sea.

He looked back along the beach; the pirates were now much closer but had to get up to where he was if they wanted to catch him. Tom was now in the water and rowing like crazy, twenty yards or so out and parallel to the beach. This part of the plan was rather flawed. The pirates were almost upon Jack but Tom was going to be a while getting along in front of the cliff. There was no other way but to jump and swim to meet the skiff. He waited till the pirates were almost at the base of the cliff, it had to be now!

Stepping back a few paces, Jack ran and leapt into mid air. The wind rushed at him as fell, he waved his arms to try to stay feet first heading into the water. He struck the water with a mighty splash and shot downwards like a diving seabird. He didn't think he was going to stop. The water was warm, like a bath. He slowed and stopped descending and began going up, helping the ascent by swimming for all he was worth.

Bursting through the surface Jack took an enormous breath and looked for Tom. There was the skiff scudding towards him. Although hampered by his clothes, he swam his most powerful strokes and closed the gap between Tom and himself. He could hear shouting from the shore, turning once he saw the pirates leaping up and down, obviously very angry that they had been thwarted. Tom stopped rowing as Jack came alongside the skiff. Jack got hold of the side of the boat and hauled himself up and over. Tom helped drag him aboard. Both out of breath they could hardly speak.

"Let's go!" panted Jack.

They sat down side by side and took up an oar each.

"Okay, let's head for the cave!"

In unison they rowed, although exhausted from all their recent strenuous exercise, they managed a decent speed. Suddenly, around the point came not one but two longboats being rowed at pace by eight men and a tillerman in each, these guys knew what they were doing and the boats were giving chase to the boys. The Captain had obviously sent more men to search for them as they were still on the island.

Panic surged through Jack and Tom, their tiring muscles were searing with pain. The pirate longboat on their left was between them and the cave and going ahead of them, the other coming up close behind. In this boat was Ned, the pirate they had heard in the cavern. He was grinning from ear to ear, a grappling hook with four hooked spikes attached to a rope in his hand.

Being cut off from the cave, the boys turned and aimed for the beach again. It would be better to attempt another escape on land rather than trying to out-row grown men.

"Come on me lads, don't be shy!" Ned pronounced shy as "shoy".

He actually had a West Country pirate accent like in a film! This bizarre thought went through Tom's mind as he and Jack kept on rowing but still expecting the inevitable. At this point four or five muskets were pointing at the boys and the pirates were laughing and cackling, obviously pleased with their work.

Jack and Tom felt panic rising as their pursuers' boats were closing in. Ned stood at the front of his boat swinging the grappling hook over his head. With a grunt he let it go and the lethal looking set of hooks flew towards the boys' skiff. It seemed to loop through the air towards them in slow motion. The steel device hit the tail of their boat and bounced into the water. Ned cursed and started to haul it in. The shock of the action seemed to spur the boys on.

Ned was too late to have another go with the grappling hook because as he finished pulling the rope back in, the boys hit the shallows, their skiff juddered to a halt as it skidded on the sand just at the waterline. Jack and Tom leapt out, starting to run as soon as they landed in the water.

Unfortunately, the pirates were ashore almost as quickly, one of their boats on each side of the skiff. Two of their pursuers were quickly onto the boys, catching them and throwing them to the ground.

"Gotcha me hearties!" Ned called out just as he was getting out of his boat.

"Well done Rafe and Jeb. Bring 'em 'ere."

The two pirates who had caught Jack and Tom hauled them to their feet and pulled them over to Ned.

"Feisty little beggars, ain't 'ee?" Ned had an evil grin on his face. "You've given us a right old runaround today. I 'ope 'ee is worth it in ransom value. Tie their 'ands and get 'em in that boat there." Ned pointed at the boat he'd been travelling in.

Rafe and Jeb, the boys didn't know who was who, manhandled them and using a couple of lengths of rope and tied their hands behind their backs. The rope was stiff and chafed their wrists. The boys were dragged into the water and bundled into the back of the boat where they sat in front of the tillerman.

"Right lads, back to The Pelican!" The front boat moved off, straightening up and then all hands rowing, surging ahead towards the pirate ship. The other boat followed a few yards behind.

Jack leant towards Tom and whispered, "Tom, our Mums and Dads will murder us!"

"I'm more worried about these guys murdering us actually."

"No, I think they will hold us to ransom, they're pirates. But who will pay a ransom? We appear to be in a different time warp or something. Worse still, our parents will think we're missing or maybe even dead!"

"Just keep calm, we will find a way to escape."

A huge slap resounded across the water as one of the pirates smacked Tom on his left ear.

"Shut up boy or I'll throw yer both to the sharks!"

Tom was almost deafened, his ear really hurt but he wasn't going to show any weakness to his captors. The boys sat in silence, heads down waiting for the next stage of this nightmare.

"Surely we're dreaming," mumbled Jack, more to himself than Tom.

The rowing boats rounded the point and there before them was the pirate ship, "The Pelican". Jack and Tom half expected Johnny Depp to be waiting on deck for them. Regardless of their fears the boys were awestruck by the sailing ship. It was amazing to think they were back in, who knows, the 1700's? Jack pondered; they hadn't had time to even begin to think about why they were here, in what was evidently a foreign land in tropical heat and in a different century. What on earth had happened to them? It had to be something to do with the cave. Perhaps it was some sort of time machine? A time cave?

Jack's reverie was interrupted by shouts from the ship. As they drew closer they could hear the buzz of loud conversation coming from what must have been the whole crew of pirates, on deck watching their approach. Tom looked on in awe and thought to himself.

"What was the expression. 'A motley crew!' That was it." He understood the expression now.

The pirates were dressed in a multitude of different clothes, many of them dressed in ragged and multi-coloured clothes.

The rowing boats pulled alongside The Pelican. A rope net had been dropped down the side of the ship and the pirates started climbing up this, making their way to the deck.

"Come on, me lads," shouted Ned, now standing up in the boat, "Rafe, untie 'em. When he's done that, my young boys, climb up that there net and get on board."

Rafe stood up behind the boys and untied the ropes. Jack and Tom rose, rubbing their hands and wrists.

"Get movin' yer little dogs!" Rafe grunted, shoving the boys hard towards the net.

Jack and Tom slammed up against the side of the ship, both grabbing the rope rungs. They dangled momentarily, their feet almost touching the water before getting a toehold and beginning the climb. The ascent was not easy, the net was floppy and the ship was moving in the water, several times the boys almost fell off. Reaching the top, two deckhands grabbed the boys and pulled them on deck.

Sprawled on their backs, Jack and Tom looked up at an absolute giant of man, dressed in classic pirate garb, a long black tunic coat, a tricorn hat and knee length boots. A large cutlass hung on his left side. A black beard covered most of his face. His large brown eyes twinkled fiercely as he gazed down at the boys.

"Well, what 'ave we got 'ere?" His voice was booming with authority. "Get up lads, let's 'ave a look at yer, then."

Jack and Tom got to their feet and stood side-by-side, fear washing over them.

"Let me introduce myself. I'm Edward Boyle, Cap'n of The Pelican. Who are yer and what are yer doin' in these waters around Pigeon Island?"

Jack was having difficulty finding his voice, it came out tremulously, "Err… I'm Jack Andrews and this is Tom Williams, we were er… out in our skiff and got pulled by the current into the cave back over there in the cliff and we ended up here. That's all we know."

"Well then we would appear to 'ave ourselves a nice little prize. We can be gettin' a message to yer Ma's and Pa's to ask them for a little thank you for findin' you lads, eh?"

"I don't think so sir," said Tom, "we're from another time dimension. We've come back in time from the twenty-first century."

"What?" Captain Boyle exclaimed. "What're yer talkin' about?"

Jack interjected, his mind racing, "We are from a time about three hundred years ahead Captain. That might seem impossible, we don't know how this has happened but it has. Look Captain, look at this," Jack took a key ring out of his pocket with a small penlight torch on it and switched it on. "Have you ever seen anything like this?"

The small torch glowed dimly; the Captain's face was unimpressed. He didn't speak. Having hung onto it since entering the cave, Tom pulled out his mobile phone. There was of course, no signal but he quickly took a picture of the Captain with the phone's camera. He said, "Look Captain." Tom held up the screen into his face.

Captain Boyle's jaw dropped looking at his own face in the picture. "What's that, magic?"

"Are you a wizard, boy? Can you do that again?"

"Better than that sir."

Tom began to sweep the phone around that ship's deck taking a video of the crew, finishing up with the Captain, all the while singing quietly the first song that came to mind, a sea shanty his Granddad used to sing to him, rather apt for their situation, Tom thought to himself.

"What shall we do with the drunken sailor? What shall we do with the drunken sailor? What shall we do with the drunken sailor, early in the mornin'."

He finished and played it back while Captain Boyle looked at the screen. The short video played back and all the while, Tom could be heard singing his song.

"Well! I'll be damned! He's a wizard all right! What else can you do boy?"

Tom's mind raced; there could be some advantage of being thought to possess powers.

"Err… I can do other magic Captain but I have to control my powers as they can be dangerous."

Captain Boyle bent down and thrust his face an inch away from Tom's. In a low growl he said, "Well now lad. I reckon that could be useful when we next plunders a Spanish ship. I want dangerous. Dangerous is good!"

Tom and Jack looked at each other and gulped.

"Take 'em to my cabin Ned and get Ralph to give 'em some bread and cheese, I'll be down soon."

Ned took the boys by the arms and led them towards a double door in the rear superstructure of the galleon. The doors were open and Ned propelled them to stairs that led to what was obviously going to be the lower deck and the Captain's cabin.

"C'mon hurry yersel's lads, we ain't got all day." Ned gave them a helping push at the top of the stairs. Jack and Tom almost danced down the steep staircase, grabbing onto the handrails at either side to steady themselves.

"In here on yer left."

Ned guided them in, hustling them through a door into a cabin about ten feet square.

There was an unmade bed against the back wall, a table in the middle of the floor with what looked like sea charts as well as dark glass bottles on it, several wooden chairs and a huge wooden cabinet which went from the floor to the ceiling with two doors on the front. Along one of the sidewalls were stacked three chests, on the rear wall were three windows with leaded lights in a diamond pattern. One of them was open slightly.

Jack and Tom looked at the chests then each other, both thinking the same thing. Treasure?

"You lads sit down there and I'll get Ralph to bring you some grub and a drink from the galley. Don't touch anythin' or ye'll regret it."

Ned disappeared through the door and they heard his feet clumping back up the stairs.

"I can't believe this is happening," Jack was incredulous, near to tears. "What's going on? Is there some sort of different dimension like we've seen in Sci-Fi films?"

"Time warp, parallel universe, whatever, who knows? But we're here and have to make the best of it until we find a way to escape," Tom was being pragmatic, putting on a bit of bravado.

"Yes, I suppose you're right. By the way, what on earth were you doing telling the Captain that you had dangerous powers? What are you going to do when he tells you to use them?"

"Err… good question. I'll have to think about that."

"Better hurry up then." Jack wasn't amused by the prospect. "Tom, let's have a quick look in these chests."

"OK, but we'd better be quick, someone might be here soon. We should hear them coming down the stairs though. Come on then."

The boys moved across the room to the chests. They simultaneously got hold of the lid of the chest which was slightly open and lifted it. What they saw made their knees go weak. The chest was full of gold and silver coins, full right to the top.

Just then, they heard feet clumping down the stairs, quickly shut the chest lid and sat in the chairs at the table. The door crashed open, banging against the large cabinet. A fat, pony-tailed man, presumably Ralph, strode in carrying two plates of something, stacked one on top of the other in one hand and two metal tankards clasped through the handles in the other.

"Right me young gentlemen, 'ere's yer grub," said the pirate. I'm Ralph the ship's cook.

"Ain't 'ee both got yerselves into a bit o' trouble now? Young boys oughta stays away from pirate ships. But never mind, old Ralph'll take care o' yer vittles needs."

Vittles? Must be food, thought both boys.

He put the dishes and tankards down with a crash. The plates had a dark looking chunk of what was obviously bread. Next to this was a dirty, yellowish grey lump of sweating substance, in which small white worm-like things which were thrashing around.

"Now then lads, get your chops around this bread and cheese and I'll see if I can find 'ee some sweetmeat from the Capn's cupboard. What's yer names, then?"

Jack and Tom's faces were a picture of disgust, looking at the food. Jack spoke first.

"I'm Jack Andrews and this is Tom Williams. Firstly sir, where are we and secondly, do you expect us to eat that, er… that whatever it is with small animals in it?"

Jack was staring in horror at the cheese. Tom was controlling a stomach heave.

"Well, bold little beggars ain't 'ee. We're on The Pelican a fine and excellent ship whose purpose is to relieve 'em Spanish hobber-nobbers o' their wealth and we're in the Spanish Main out of Jamaica. Them small animals as ye say are just maggots. That's like an extra meat ration. Gerrit down 'ee lads, yer'll love it." He cackled with laughter.

Ralph turned to the large cabinet and opened one of the doors.

"What we got 'ere then," Ralph mumbled to himself as he browsed the shelves. "Nuthin' that's what we got, Capn's scoffed the lot 'imself. Don't worry lads. I'll go back to the galley and bring ye some sweetmeats."

With that, Ralph disappeared through the cabin door and up the stairs. Without speaking, both boys picked up the pewter plates the food was on and rushed to the window at the back of the cabin. Slightly ajar already, they flung it wide open and tipped out the bread and cheese. Before it hit the water below two seagulls had caught the cheese.

"The Spanish Main, Jamaica, that's the Caribbean! Jack, come on let's jump we can swim ashore and try to get back." Tom couldn't contain himself.

"OK, let's go."

There were two windows that opened, one either side of a solid fixed window. Jack opened the other window and the boys started to climb through, getting a leg each over sill. Just then they heard footfall on the stairs, Ralph, or someone, was on his way back.

"Quick back to the table, it's no good," whispered Tom.

The boys scrambled back to the table as Ralph's fat jolly face peered round the cabin door.

"Finished already? You lads must have been half starved. Enjoy it then?"

"Err… yes Ralph, thank you, really nice once you got into it."

"Good lads, now try some of this," Ralph said as he pulled a large cork stopper from a stone pottery jar. He poured a dark brown sticky mass onto the empty plates and produced two very primitive-looking spoons from his waistband and dropped them on the table.

The boy's thoughts were immediate and the same. Those spoons had been nestling against Ralph's fat sweating belly. Yuck! They picked up the spoons and wiped them on their Tee shirts and each tentatively took a spoonful of the brown mess. Up to their lips they tasted a tiny amount. Sweet, very sweet.

"Not bad!" exclaimed Tom. "Yes, quite yummy!"

Jack and Tom wolfed the food down. They were much hungrier than they thought as Ralph had predicted earlier. It was obviously some sort of fruit in sickly, syrupy goo.

"What is this Ralph?" queried Jack as he put down his spoon having swallowed the last mouthful.

"Well, that's fermented berries or cherries or somethin' like that, with molasses. I shot a large bird meself on the island this morning and cut it open and them there berries were in its belly. They had softened up nicely, don't 'ee think?"

Tom beat Jack marginally to the windows where they both heaved up the berries. Again swooping seabirds caught some of the mess before it hit the sea.

"What's goin' on with ye lads? Are ye seasick? We not even be sailin'."

"Ohhh!" Tom moaned. Jack wasn't far behind with his groan. "That's gross Ralph! Giving us food from the gut of a bird!"

"That me lad was a special treat I give 'ee 'cos I feels sorry for 'ee. Well don't be lookin' fer ought else cos there ain't any, apart from rat stew I'm doin' fer the crew tonight." Ralph laughed uproariously again.

"Ralph, we're so sorry but we're just not used to this sort of food. We're from err… somewhere else where we eat different stuff like pasta, pizza, hamburgers, things like that."

"Never heard o' that, ye'll just have to have rat stew tonight with the rest of the crew." Heh heh heh, Ralph's chuckle was mischievous and he had a twinkle in his eye.

The boys gulped in unison. Tonight seemed too soon to test their delicate stomachs. They picked up the tankards and drank the brackish water, which could have been worse but was better than nothing. At that, they heard another set of boots banging down the stairs. Captain Boyle entered the cabin doffed his hat and bowed to the boys.

"Welcome aboard lads. I hope you are bein' well taken care of by Ralphie here?"

Jack spoke up, "Captain, you really must let us go, our parents will be worried, they'll have the police out looking for us."

"Aahh yes, yer parents. Yer Ma's and Pa's. Well, they can wait. I've got plans fer 'ee when we encounter the next Spanish ship, loaded with treasure. We needs some of yer magic young Tom. Eh lad?"

Tom glanced down at his feet and mumbled, "Yes Captain, but I'm not sure my magic will be any good with any sort of err… battle."

"Oh yes it will lad, ye'll do as I say. I'm the Cap'n o' this 'ere ship. Ralphie, take 'em to Jasper, he's in the armoury. They can work their passage as powder boys. Tell 'im to give these boys some work, keep 'em busy till supper time." At that he left the cabin and stomped up the stairs.

"Follow me lads," said Ralph in his cheery tones. He didn't seem to have a care in the world.

"Perhaps he's mad," Jack thought to himself.

Two

They followed Ralph up the stairs and walked outside into the fierce tropical sun. Out on deck, seamen were coiling ropes, sharpening cutlasses and daggers and loading pistols and muskets. Jack and Tom had seen these routines in many a movie.

"I'm just waiting for Captain Jack Sparrow to appear," said Jack rather wistfully.

"Wish he would and at least we would know that where we are and what we're doing is just make believe. This is real Jack!"

Ralph led the boys to a square trap in the deck towards the front of the ship. Pulling on a ring, he heaved open the trap door and started down a set of steep stairs. Jack and Tom followed hanging onto the side handrail, as the steps were more like a ladder. At the bottom Ralph headed straight ahead to a barred gate that looked like a prison cell door.

"Open up Jasper, I've got some company fer 'ee."

Jasper walked slowly forward from the depths of what they learned was the armoury. This was the young man who had found Jack in the cavern and hadn't given the game away. He turned a key and the door swung outwards towards the boys.

"Come in gentlemen," he said in a quiet well-spoken voice. "Let's see what we can find for you to do."

He stepped back as Tom followed by Jack walked inside. Jasper locked the door behind them. Ralph turned and walked off with a happy grin and a departing cheery, "See yers at supper lads."

"It was you who found us in that cave, wasn't it? You risked your safety by not giving us away. Thank you for that." Tom was gracious in his thanks. Jack joined in thanking Jasper too.

"It's a pity that you didn't stay hidden on Pigeon Island and you might have got away."

"Well, we thought they might be bringing more crew onto the island to look for us. Nothing we can do about that now." Jack was putting on a brave face when really he was thinking, "If only."

"Now then, what are your names? What are you doing getting yourselves caught up with this lot and putting yourselves at great risk?" Jasper's voice was accent-less and nothing like the pirates.

They introduced themselves, then Jack asked what year it was and when Jasper told them it was 1720, both boys shook their heads in disbelief. After a pause to let that information sink in, they told their tale, both chipping in with what they thought was an important part. However, going through their story they could see the incredulous look spread across Jasper's face. In the telling, Jack and Tom could understand that no one was likely to believe that they had come from another time dimension.

Jasper waited until they had finished their tale of woe and spoke up. "Well boys, I can't say that I understand about you living in Cornwall three hundred years in the future but what I do know is that you, like my sister and I, are at the mercy of these brutes until we can escape. I am Jasper Bennett, aged fifteen years, son of Sir James Bennett who owns a sugar plantation on Jamaica. My sister Kathryn, or Kate as we know her, both attend school in England. Kathryn is thirteen. We were on board the English ship, 'The Golden Lion,' a year ago, on our way to Jamaica to visit our father when we were attacked by The Pelican."

Jasper's voice caught with emotion as he went on, "Almost all our crew and the other travellers were slaughtered by these animals. Our ship was set on fire and sank. They took Kate and me prisoner and sent my father a ransom letter. My father paid the ransom of ten thousand guineas but they cheated him and have demanded more money. At this point I don't think my father has paid again. We don't know what's going on. Boyle keeps Kate locked in a small cabin below decks. I do as I'm told and they seem to trust me. However, they know that I can't escape or do anything that would endanger Kate."

"And you've been with these pirates for a year?" Jack's voice rose to almost a squeak.

"I regret to say yes. While they keep Kate locked up, there's absolutely nothing we can do. She is allowed on deck when we are at sea, where there is no chance of escape. I fear for her safety because these bloodthirsty rapscallions are always on the lookout for other ships to plunder. It's so dangerous for all of us!"

Jack and Tom didn't know what a rapscallion was but they could guess.

Jack's brain was racing. "Look Jasper, we should get a plan together and we can help each other escape. Do you know where we are heading for next?"

"The Spaniards more often than not use one of their own colonies, such as the island of Hispaniola. But since England's war with Spain ended, they sometimes use Jamaica as a stop off port from South America before crossing the Atlantic back to Spain because it has better docking facilities and supplies.

So the pirates sail around the waters to the west of Jamaica, waiting for a Spanish treasure ship. When they want a safe haven, they go to Tortola, it's a British sugar plantation colony in what Columbus named the Virgin Islands. It's run by slavemasters and it's a haven for pirates too. I expect if this lot have some luck plundering a Spanish ship, Tortola is where we'll be heading which is a long way from Jamaica and our father's home."

"Oh no!" exclaimed Tom.

"Well if we manage to get out of that alive, what are the chances of escaping from Tortola?" Tom's voice was hopeful.

"Not good, we would have to get to the English authorities. They may take some convincing about who we are. The place is overrun with pirates who wouldn't think twice about slitting our throats if we were considered a threat to them and their brethren. Our best option is to escape and then find an English ship en-route to Jamaica and see if they will give us passage."

"Well, if that's the best option we should consider it, what do you think Tom?"

"I'll try anything to get us home Jack, this whole thing is bizarre, crazy, like a bad dream."

"Gentlemen," Jasper said, "we can try to find another opportunity to discuss escape but I must give you some work, no one on this ship can be idle. Here, let me show you how to make up the powder charges for the guns."

Jasper opened a barrel and pointing at the black substance inside, said, "This is gunpowder and we put it into these cloth bags." He pulled out a cylindrical shaped bag from a wooden box and held it up for the boys to see. Using a wooden scoop he ladled the fine black powder into the bag until it was full. He then tied a cord, closing up the bag.

"What are they used for Jasper?" asked Tom.

"These are pushed into the cannon by one of the gun crew. The cannonball is then rammed in and a bundle of straw pushed in as wadding to hold the ball in. The gunner pushes a spike through a hole at the back of the gun to puncture the bag and then he pours some gunpowder down the hole. He then lights the powder with what they call a slow match, which is a piece of burning rope. This small charge of powder ignites the main charge and BANG! The cannonball flies out of the gun barrel. The cannonballs this ship uses weigh thirty-two pounds, and will destroy the side-timbers of a ship at two hundred yards. At greater distances they will destroy superstructure on the top of the ship, masts, sails, raised cabins and of course kill anyone who happens to be in the way, more often than not with the splintered wood shattered by the cannonball."

"So we are actually helping the pirates to kill other people by doing this," reflected Tom.

Both boys pondered this but concluded they had no choice in the matter. Jasper dropped his head and just gave a slight nod of agreement.

"Right, how many do you want filled?"

"Just keep going till you're told to stop. That will be at sunset. Then you will start again tomorrow."

"Have you been doing this on your own?" asked Tom.

"Well, yes but only since we stopped off at Cuba a few days ago and the two powder boys they had working here managed to escape."

"Oh, then it is possible to escape," responded Tom.

"Yes, but those boys had no families and didn't care where they were. We have to be rather more selective where we get off."

"Yes, hmmm… yes, I suppose you're right," said Jack.

"Anyway, Jack, Tom, Ned the Bosun is next in command and he runs the crew. He will be expecting a good day's work from us so we keep going until food time."

"Can't wait for supper if it's anything like lunch!" Tom was at his most sarcastic.

The boys set to the task, one of them holding the bag the other ladling in the gunpowder. It was a simple, boring job. They held the bags over the open barrel to catch any gunpowder which spilled over.

Jack looked up after a while, addressing Jasper. "How many sea battles have you been involved in Jasper? Have you helped these guys kill innocent people?"

"Guys? Does that mean Pirates?" Queried Jasper.

"No Jasper, it means 'men' and it's slang, a sort of nickname," replied Jack.

"Nickname?"

"Oh, please Jasper, we'll be doing this all day! It's an expression where we live and in our time period."

Jasper shook his head in puzzlement and replied to the question.

"Yes, unfortunately on two occasions, and I lent them no hand in it. I locked myself here in the powder store."

He returned to the musket he was cleaning and the boys continued filling the bags. Lost in deep thought, each boy was carrying out his task robotically. They talked infrequently and only then to discuss something about the job at hand. Their thoughts were about their families and how terrified their parents would be. Jasper's father knew pirates had kidnapped him; Jack and Tom's parents had no idea where they were. This was just awful. They just had to escape.

After an hour or so they could hear shouting from the deck. Jasper told the boys that they were about to set sail and indeed, within a short time they could feel the ship moving, creaking and groaning with the swell of the waves. Filling the bags became rather more difficult now as the rise and fall of the ship made for less precision for the boys.

Weary beyond measure, they could see sunset was approaching as diminishing light was coming in the small portholes. This meant they could stop work soon. Jasper dashed their hopes of an early finish when he told them that there was more to be done before they were finished. He explained that the bags they had filled had to be taken to the gun deck.

Placing about twenty bags into a canvas carrier rather like a hammock, they took a rope attached at each end and lifted the very heavy load between them. Leading them up a level, Jasper brought Jack and Tom onto the gun deck which for the boys was awe inspiring. There must have been twenty guns on each side of the ship, each one in front of a gun port. This was an opening with a flap, a sort of vertical trapdoor of wood covering the gun port. Around each gun were three or four rough-looking crewmen who started whistling and jeering as soon as they saw the boys.

"What ho me hearties! What 'andsome young boys!"

"Shaddup! Leave 'em be!" The catcalling stopped immediately. It was Ned.

"Right me lads, you've got powder bags. Come with me."

Ned took them to the last gun at the forward part of the ship and showed them where to put the bags. This was into large, open half barrels, in position next to each cannon.

"Five in each barrel, I 'ope you've got plenty more down in the powder store? Bring 'em up and give 'em out at five a barrel until ye've done."

"Yes sir," said Jack.

He knew that it was going to take several trips until they were done. Indeed that was the case as it took them about another hour of back and forth carrying and distributing the gunpowder bags to the guns.

Feeling absolutely exhausted and fretting over their situation, the boys didn't feel too good when it came to eating. They had been told by Ned to go to the galley and pick up a plate and Ralph would give them supper.

"I really don't feel like eating the rubbish I'm sure Ralph is going to give us," moaned Tom.

"I know, but we should eat to keep our strength up. Come on, let's give it a try." Jack was trying to be upbeat and positive.

On the way to the galley, they met Jasper coming down from the main deck. He said he was on his way to supper to and would show them the routine. Passing through a sort of dining area with rough tables and benches, many of the crew were seated, stuffing their faces with what looked like meat and vegetables. The conversation died and all eyes were raised to watch the boys go by. Jack and Tom felt distinctly uncomfortable. Reaching what was a sort of hatch between the eating area and what they could only guess was the kitchen. Before them they could see cooking pots with food in them on top of a huge iron stove which was standing on flat stone slabs. A chain from each corner of the stove was attached to the huge ceiling beams. These were, Tom thought, presumably to steady it in rough seas.

There were knives, chopping blocks, ladles and cooking implements of all shapes and sizes lying around on top of work surfaces and cupboards. An eighteenth century kitchen on a ship.

They stood behind Jasper who handed them each a metal plate, which Tom suggested must be pewter; and a wooden spoon, which Jack suggested must be made of wood. That brought a smile at last to Tom's face.

Ralph the cook, was beaming as usual. "Here lads, get yer chops around this," he said with his sing-song accent. "We've got goat stew and bread. We shot some wild goats on pigeon island this mornin'. Fresh meat, makes a nice change from salt pork and pickled beef. Funny that, I've never seen a pigeon on Pigeon Island. Should be Goat Island!" Ralph was amusing himself yet again and roared with laughter. He put a slice of rock hard bread onto each of the plates and ladled the stew on top of it.

"The gravy will soften that bread, yer'll think yer mammies made it. It's bootiful!"

The boys made their way to a table where two pirates were sitting finishing their food.

One of them was in his twenties. Jack thought to himself that the other was ten or more years older, but it was difficult as they were tanned dark brown by the tropical sun and covered in a layer of what was probably dirt. The three boys slid onto hard wooden benches keeping their gaze cast down, not wanting to look the pirates in the eye.

"Well now, laddies. What are ye doin' in these parts without yer mama's and papa's?" The older pirate was staring straight at Jack.

Not wanting to go through the story Jack decided to just give some bare bones in the hope it would satisfy the man's curiosity.

"Err... we were in our skiff doing some fishing and got too far out. We tried to row back but the tide was too strong to row against and found ourselves adrift at sea. That's when we got chased and caught by you pirates."

"Well, not quite the story I 'eard but near enough. I 'eard ye gave Ned and his boys a merry dance on the island. Anythin' that upsets old Ned is music to my ears."

The pirate was grinning, showing yellow teeth, some of which were missing. He let out a laugh like a hyena.

"I'm Ezra and this 'ere is Ben. He said, pointing to the younger pirate next to him. If ye've got any silver, gold or trinkets to give us, we'll look after 'ee. There be some dangerous men around 'ere."

"I'm afraid not sir," replied Tom.

"Then what about them funny lookin' bracelets on yer arms?" Ned was staring at the boy's digital watches with black plastic straps.

"These are worthless, as you can see they are just black err... not even leather, no gold or silver." Jack replied.

"Then I hope ye makes it to next week then!" He cackled uproariously and stood to leave the table. Ben did the same and as he stood he locked his glance on Jack.

In a chilling voice, he hissed, "Take care boys, say yer prayers at night won't 'ee?"

The two men walked away towards the stairs, laughing as they went.

Jasper joined the boys and Jack looked across at him, "What was that all about Jasper?" Jack asked as the two pirates left the dining area.

Jasper leaned forward, looking very intense.

"They're bullies and very dangerous men, they enjoy picking on younger crew. Stay away from them."

The boys tentatively tasted the stew, the meat was a bit chewy but not unlike the taste of roast lamb their mothers did for Sunday lunch some weekends. They tucked in, they were half starved, not having eaten for hours; that is apart from the meal they had thrown up. Even the soggy bread tasted good. There were potatoes in it too which helped fill their empty stomachs.

Jasper went and got them all water to drink, which he ladled from a barrel into ancient-looking flagons. Jack and Tom drank the water, washing down the stew. They hadn't realised how thirsty they were.

The eating area had cleared leaving only the three boys. Ralph came over with the stew pot and gave them each another ladle full of stew and more bread. The boys made short work of it and soon were handing back their plates which they had mopped clean to Ralph, who dropped them into a barrel full of water, which had a layer of grease and food leftovers floating on the surface.

"Blimey Tom! Can't say much for the hygiene around here."

"We've got more to worry about than hygiene. Jack."

Jasper looked curiously at the boys, "Hygiene, what's that?"

"Don't worry about it Jasper," said Tom, "just something about keeping things clean and germ free which we do where we come from."

"Germ free?"

"Really Jasper, it doesn't matter." Tom didn't fancy giving a lesson in germ theory. Biology wasn't one of his best subjects.

Tom looked at Jack and shook his head. "This is incredible and depressing at the same time Jack. How on earth did we get here and are we really going to be able to escape?"

Emotion coursed through his voice, he was almost crying but didn't want to embarrass himself. He bit his lower lip and looked down at the table.

"Well, if we don't try, we won't know." Jack wanted to sound positive but he didn't feel it.

Jasper having had similar emotional turmoil, knew what the boys were going through. Homesick, fearing for their lives, a whole list of worries and concerns as well as having to survive amongst these villains every day.

He stood up to break the moment and said, "Gentlemen, let us to bed."

They climbed the stairs to the middle deck where the sleeping quarters were. Following behind Jasper, Jack and Tom entered the low-beamed area. Hammocks were slung from what was the horizontal ship's planking to upright timbers. Many of the hammocks were occupied by sailors in differing states of repose. Some were smoking pipes, some were asleep, one was playing a concertina-like instrument and others just lay with their eyes open starting at the ceiling timbers. The smell of sweaty, unwashed bodies was overpowering. Loud farts emanated from several different directions. Jasper led the boys to two hammocks side by side. He motioned towards them with his right hand.

"I know these two are free because the former occupants were killed in the last action we had. Both stabbed by the other ship's captain who was very 'andy with his sword."

Jack and Tom's mouths fell open at the same time.

"Do we have to sleep in the hammocks of dead men?"

"Well I don't think they can hurt you now, do you? Besides, they are the only empty ones."

"What happened to the captain who killed these men?" Queried Tom.

"Captain Boyle took off his head with his cutlass from behind."

The boys just gulped, their eyes wide.

"I can't see we've any option but to sleep here Tom."

Jasper left them and walked over to a hammock a short distance away and climbed in. Tom looked at the hammock that he was standing in front of; it was about three feet off the floor. He lifted one leg into it, hung onto the rope that was tied to an iron ring and launched his other leg into the canvas. In a split second he had spun over the top and crashed onto the deck. Jack and several other sailors who had been watching thought it hilarious. Embarrassed but not daunted it took Tom three goes to get into the hammock.

Bruised but triumphant, lying on his back he said, "Right Jack, you smarty pants, let's see you do it!"

Jack smiled and looked around and everyone was looking at him.

"No pressure then!"

Hanging onto the header rope, he leapt up, both feet off the floor as if he were going to vault right over the hammock. He twisted in the air and landed smack on his back in the canvas, the hammock swung to and fro like a pendulum but Jack was safe, he wasn't going to tip out. There was a small cheer from the watching pirates, who when the fun was over, quickly went back to their conversations or pipe smoking.

"Huh! Tom exclaimed, "beginner's luck!"

"A well planned and executed operation Tom. Keep your eye on me, I know what I'm doing." Jack was being smug.

"Then you'd better think about how we can escape from this ship. I'll keep my eye on you then!" whispered Tom.

"We'll start working on it while we're filling gunpowder packets tomorrow," responded Jack, yawning. It had been a long day. Both boys were truly exhausted. And within moments they were fast asleep.

Three

"OUT O' YER BEDS YE USELESS PACK OF SCUM! WAKE UP! WAKE UP! LET'S BE 'AVIN' YOU THEN! GET UP ON DECK NOW! COME ON GET MOVING!"

A dull clanging noise accompanied this shouting. The boys were rudely shocked out of deep slumber. It was Ned. He was a tough, no nonsense character who kept the ship's company in order. He was banging a short solid-looking piece of wood called a belaying pin, on a metal food plate. Bodies began tumbling out of their hammocks fully dressed and heading towards the stairs.

Jack and Tom half fell, half climbed, out of their hammocks and followed the pack. The air on deck was warm but refreshing compared to the fug below in the sleeping quarters. It wasn't quite daylight yet but a faint pink and orange glow was discernible on the horizon. The sea had a slight swell running and the fresh breeze was making the sails billow. The ship appeared to be moving along at a fair pace. With the rising sun ahead of them, they were obviously heading east.

Some of the pirates stood in a crowd below the raised half deck at the rear of the ship. Many of them stood in a line along the sides of the ship peeing overboard. Captain Boyle stood while waiting for the crew to assemble. Satisfied they were all present after a nod from Ned, he began to speak.

"Right you greedy dogs. We're 'eading to the area between Hispaniola and Jamaica where in both o' them places some of the Spaniards stop off to stock up with some grub and water before they sail back to Spain. We're goin' to be lookin' for a stray ship workin' outside a Flota, thinkin' they can make a dash into the Atlantic without bein' spotted. We'll be relievin' those Spanish dandies of their treasure."

A cheer went up from the crew. Many of them were beaming with excitement. Some of them looked plain evil with smiles that Jack thought looked like something from a horror movie.

Captain Boyle's eyes were alight with passion as he carried on, "When we find a Spaniard, I want ruthless fightin' from 'ee. I want the fear of God put into their crews and passengers so we can take their ship quickly without too much loss to us."

Addressing the gun crews, he went on, "Gunners, I'm relyin' on 'ee to keep a constant rate of fire goin', not less than two rounds every five minutes from every gun crew. I want their heads spinnin' with gunfire so we can get alongside and board 'em before 'ey knows what's 'appenin' to 'em. I want their crew to be dispatched quickly and efficiently. All hands are to have every available weapon nearby from now until we find a Spaniard. ARE WE READY FOR THE FIGHT BOYS?"

A huge cry went up from all on deck, "AYE CAP'N!"

"Ned, get this lot to work, set the compass, I want us two nautical miles east of Hispaniola and let's get there as quick as we can."

"Aye, aye Cap'n." Ned started calling out orders, none of which meant anything to the boys. The crew ran to their various posts, some climbing rigging, some back to their gun deck others to whatever their jobs were.

Tom turned to Jasper and asked, "What's a Flota?"

"The Spanish have been shipping treasures and gold from South America to Spain for almost three hundred years. A

Flota is a group of ships, a treasure fleet, which sail together to protect each other from pirates and English privateers who are constantly on the lookout for a prize. It's said that the vast wealth they have stolen from the natives is becoming less, so some ships make the journey across the Atlantic on their own. Captain Boyle looks for those."

Both boys were overwhelmed by an emotion that they had never really felt before, fear for their lives. This was not the feeling that one got when driving with Mum or Dad and an idiot in another car almost caused a crash. Or the fear one got when doing something daring or risky. This was pit of the stomach stuff, "I could be killed or maimed in a bloody battle where people are fighting for their lives."

The boy's thoughts were interrupted when the Captain boomed, "You boys come to my cabin. Now!"

Jack and Tom's hearts sank. They could hardly put one foot in front of the other as they made their way down the stairs to the captain's cabin.

"This is it Tom," whimpered Jack, "you're going to have to show him some magic! What are you going to do?"

"I've been thinking about it, I have something up my sleeve, I hope it will work."

Jack gulped hard. "I hope so too!"

They reached the Captain's cabin and knocked on the door.

"Come boys, come in, come in."

They stepped in and looked tentatively at the Captain seated behind his table which was still covered in charts, dividers and a device the boys knew to be a sextant, used for taking readings of angles of the sun, moon and stars to calculate positions on the earth.

"Sit, sit lads. 'ow're ye bein' treated? Well, I 'ope? We makin' pirates of 'ee yet?" With that he burst into booming laughter.

The boys grinned, more like grimaces, as they pulled out two huge oak chairs, which were so heavy they could hardly slide them out to sit on them.

"Now then, Tom aint it? Let's 'ear 'bout yer magic. Where's yer magic box? What're yer goin' to do to 'elp us take a Spaniard when we sees 'im?"

"Well Captain, my magic box has something called a satellite navigation system which will allow us to plot where the Spanish ships are."

Jack's head shot around, his eyes and mouth wide open at the ridiculous lie Tom had just told the pirate. They were three hundred years back in time; there were no satellites, no mobile phone masts and no network signal. Even if there had been he couldn't plot where another ship was going to be unless his phone had radar as a feature. What was Tom thinking? He was going to get them keelhauled, fifty lashes at the masthead or walking the plank or whatever dreadful punishment pirates issued to mutineers or wrongdoers. It was going to take an unlikely coincidence for a Spanish ship to actually be where Tom predicted it would be.

"Right, Tom lad, here's my chart," Captain Boyle stood up and pulled a huge sea chart sideways on the table so Tom could look at it. "This is where we are now," he indicated with one of the points of what the boys knew as dividers, "and this is where we're sailin' towards." Boyle pointed just to the west of the island of Hispaniola. "Now where and when do ye reckon we can catch a Spaniard?"

Tom pulled his mobile out of his pocket and switched it on. The battery strength was still showing almost full as he had charged it overnight before their adventure had started and apart from the pantomime on deck when they were first captured, hadn't used it. Could that have only been two days ago since they stepped into their skiff at Mennan Cove? It felt like a month. He pressed a few keys and opened up the calculator programme and did a calculation. He could feel the sweat running down his back and a sick feeling in his stomach as he made a performance of hitting the keys.

"Well Captain, my magic box predicts that we will sight a Spanish treasure ship here at err… mid-afternoon in two days time."

Tom picked up the dividers and stuck the point into the chart slightly to the east of Jamaica. Tom was getting carried away. Jack kept quiet and stared straight ahead. Captain Boyle picked up quill pen and dipped it into an inkpot on the table. He wrote down in a large diary-like book what Jack and Tom could only guess were chart coordinates.

"Are ye sure lad? Is that thing accurate? Is your… magic box workin'? We can't be wastin' time sailin' around waitin' for a ship that might not appear this side of Christmas!"

"Yes sir, although I am aware that sailors have had problems plotting longitude for centuries." Tom had watched a Discovery Channel television programme some time ago about a man called Harrison who invented a chronometer which was a watch about as big as an alarm clock, which enabled a much more accurate means of plotting longitude.

"This is a magic box from the future which will plot our position within a few hundred feet. However, it can be affected by bad weather."

The more he said the more Tom backed himself into a corner. He was taking a bit of a risk here, trying to confuse the issue and hopefully use the weather as an excuse when they arrived at the predicted spot and didn't see a Spanish ship. He just had to pray for bad weather. Jack rolled his eyes and shook his head. He couldn't believe what he was hearing.

"Tom, Tom, lad what are ye sayin' 'ere? That yer magic box is magic enough to tell us where and when we can find a Spaniard but not magic enough when the weather is a bit inclement? I think yer tryin' to mislead old Edward Boyle, ain't 'ee?" He had a smile on his face but it was not a pleasant one. More like a tiger when it was settling down to eat a deer it had just caught.

"No Captain!" Tom's heart was racing and his brain was in overdrive. His glib, or so he thought, clever plan was falling apart. He struggled to recapture some high ground.

"Err, my magic box, is er, accurate from the time period we came from and live in, but here, three hundred years behind it's not so accurate." He and Jack both knew he was waffling, just saying what came into his head. The Captain appeared to think so too.

"Sounds like yer box ain't so magic after all, eh Tom? Maybe I should just throw the two of 'ee and yer magic box overboard. Any reason why I shouldn't?"

Jack, for the first time since they arrived in the Captain's cabin, interjected.

"At least give us the benefit of the doubt Captain, please. If we sail there and we don't find a Spanish treasure ship then you can do what you like with us and no doubt you will. Please just give us a chance to prove Tom is right." Jack was buying time.

Edward Boyle stared at Jack. He was looking but not really seeing, it was a trance like gaze and he was deep in thought. After what seemed ages he glared at each of the boys and said,

"Right lads. It was my intention to sail to that area anyway. I suppose we 'ave nothing to lose in followin' the plan I would have undertaken' if 'ee both wasn't 'ere. If what 'ee says is right then it's a bonus, ain't that right, lads? I'm sure 'ee both agree with old Edward eh?"

His smile was back. It made the boys feel very vulnerable and wobbly inside.

In unison they replied, "Yes Captain!"

"Right, get out of my sight. Go see Ralph and get some grub then quick as 'ee like, get back to the armoury and get plenty of powder packets made up." Boyle looked down at his chart. They were dismissed. The boys stood up and left the cabin.

On the stairs up to the deck Jack swung around to Tom.

"What on earth were you thinking about you nutcase? Why couldn't you just have said your 'magic box' couldn't help? Why did you have to make it worse by saying WHEN we would sight a Spanish treasure ship? We are in even deeper trouble now, you idiot!"

"I thought it was a good idea Jack. I was trying to buy time and get us closer to Jamaica where hopefully we can escape and get to Jasper's father for help. It wasn't till I heard the words coming out of my mouth that I realised how idiotic I was being. It was too late by then. I'm so sorry."

"But what did you expect to gain?"

"I thought he might be kinder to us if he thought we were useful to him – rather than just ransom material."

"That's pathetic Tom. You should have discussed your bright idea with me and I would have told you how stupid it was. Anyway, we have to live with it now."

They made their way across the deck to stairs at the front of the ship, which led them to the galley. Entering the galley, it was empty apart from Ralph and his helper, Isaac, an older man who appeared to have a permanent limp. He was scraping plates and bowls of scraps of food, presumably from the rest of the crew who had all had breakfast while the boys were with the Captain. There was a pleasant food smell all around which reminded them of baking bread.

"Mornin' to yer lads. 'ow be 'ee? Want some grub do 'ee? Sit down over there and I'll fetch 'ee somethin'."

It was evident that for whatever reason, Ralph had taken a shine to the boys. He went back into the kitchen and busied himself as the boys sat at the nearest table. They just sat and didn't speak. Tom was mortified for worsening their situation, Jack was really mad at him for the same reason.

There they sat for ten minutes, staring ahead of them, silent, thinking about home, their predicament and what was facing them. Possibly death by Spanish sailors or soldiers. Killed by a cannonball, musket ball, sword or cutlass. Stabbed by some dagger-wielding maniac who was fighting for his life. Or thrown overboard because of Tom's stupid idea.

Their deep thought was disturbed by Ralph's approach. He was holding a pewter plate in each hand and he put them down in front of the boys.

"There y'are lads, get yer gums around that!" He was grinning ear to ear.

In front of Jack and Tom was a plate with slices of what looked like ham, the kind their parents bought at a deli. What was it called again? Jack had it, that's right, Parma ham. These slices were much thicker though and looked delicious. Next to that was a fried egg and what was obviously freshly made bread. These were flat, round pieces of bread about half an inch thick. Ralph made this bread by dropping the flattened dough made from flour and water into a large frying pan where it cooked and the result was a bit like Indian naan bread. Alongside on their plates were some pieces of pineapple.

"Wow Ralph! This is wonderful," exclaimed Tom.

"Fantastic!" said Jack.

Ralph beamed, "That be 'am collected from a Spanish ship. They 'ad no further use fer it!" he screeched with laughter. Ralph loved his own jokes.

The boys made short work of the food; they were, as usual, starving. Clean plates were pushed away from them and they sat back.

"Ralph, that was delicious," said Tom, "but what sort of egg was that, it tasted err… a bit fishy?"

"Gulls eggs me lad, collected them meself from the cliffs when we was ashore on Pigeon Island. Yer know, maybe it should have been called Seagull Island, as there ain't no Pigeons there. Heh heh heh!" He was at it again.

"Oh! Right, how nice," Tom's voice tailed off. Jack said nothing but he didn't think it was too bad at all. They were going to have to eat whatever was put in front of them to keep up their strength.

"Right lads, off 'ee go to work, Jasper will be waitin for 'ee in the armoury. Make sure 'ee get those powder packets right, don't want our balls droppin' short, do we." He screeched with hysterical laughter. He thought he was hilarious.

The boys put on a little giggle to humour Ralph and set off back to the armoury. As they arrived, Jasper was just coming out and about to lock the barred door.

"Ah, here you are, I've been waiting."

"Yes, sorry we've not been here to help, we had to see the Captain so we were late for breakfast. Where are you going Jasper?" enquired Jack.

"The Captain said I can talk to Kate before they let her on deck to stretch her legs and get some air."

"Are you going to tell Kate about us and that we're planning to escape at some point?" asked Tom.

"Of course. She has to know so when we've come up with a plan we can keep her informed.

"Good, I hope she's Okay," said Jack.

"OK? What does that mean? Jasper looked puzzled.

Jack realised that the expression probably hadn't been around in 1720. "It means alright, good, fine."

"Ah, right then, I mean Okay!" They all laughed. Jasper continued, looking serious now, "Just get on with filling the powder packets and distribute them to the guns, like you did yesterday. It's in our interests to make sure that any ships we attack, we win the battle. The guns usually decide the outcome by inflicting damage and many casualties before the crew board the other ship and take on the Spaniards hand to hand. I know that makes us accomplices in death but providing sufficient quantities of powder packets helps us win, rather than the opposition defeating us. We have no idea how we would be treated by our conquerors."

The enormity of what they were involved in was sinking in quickly with the boys. They were part of a real life war in which people were going to die and they were going to be instrumental in helping that happen. Jasper turned and left Jack and Tom to their thoughts.

"I hate this Tom," Jack said, the emotion coming through in his voice. "What can we do?"

"Nothing till we come up with a decent escape plan. We're stuck here until then."

Jack sat on the barrel he had used yesterday and started filling the bags with gunpowder. Tom sighed in resignation and joined him, sitting opposite on another barrel. Jasper rejoined them after a half-hour or so in lighter spirits. He explained to them that he'd been able to spend some time alone with Kate. He had told her about Jack and Tom which had brought a little hope to her. She felt that with four of them now involved they might be able to escape. She and Jasper weren't sure how, but they felt that strength in numbers was a positive thing. She could not, however, understand the time-travel part of the story. The boys weren't surprised, they didn't either.

Back and forward to the gun deck was tedious and hard physical work but they kept going. It was hot, humid and smelly on the ship and it was evident that bathing was not something that pirates in the 1700's did on a regular basis. They reeked of body odour and other accumulated smells. Their teeth were yellow and in some cases, non existent. Their clothes were dirty and shabby. Jack thought a dip in the sea fully clothed might resolve some of those problems for a little while.

The day seemed endless, they stopped for a few minutes and were given a piece of the mouldy cheese and Ralph's flatbread that Jasper collected from the galley. It did appear that Ralph had chosen the best bits of cheese for them. They drank only brackish water from a barrel. By sunset they were absolutely done in, too tired to eat but knew they should.

They made their way to the galley. Ralph, as usual, was grinning as he greeted them. "Hey ho, me lads! 'Ow're yer doin'? Been getting' us ready for action 'ave 'ee?"

Ralph's continually cheerful mood was infectious and both boys felt it would be wrong to start moaning.

"Yes Ralph, we're fully-fledged powder boys now, I think if anyone approached us with a flame we would explode," Jack pointed to their clothes, ingrained with powder, their hands and finger nails black.

Ralph roared with laughter. "There's a bowl of hot water in the galley, Isaac will show 'ee. Go and wash yer 'ands and come back I've got another little treat for 'ee."

The boys went to where Isaac, Ralph's helper was and he directed them to the bowl of water. The boys were delighted to get some of the muck and gunpowder off their hands. They could taste it because they had been breathing it in all day. They returned to Ralph who with Isaac was now doling out the same sort stew as they had had for supper the previous evening.

"Yer goin' to 'ave to wait until we've finished feedin' the crew, lads. Just sit and wait round there."

The boys sat on a bench to one side of the hatch through which the food was served, if you could call it served, more like slopped. They watched as the pirates stuffed their food down from their plates using wooden spoons. Some of them left quickly after eating, others hung around smoking foul smelling pipes. Before long, the air was thick with smoke.

As they sat the two mean-looking characters from last evening, Ezra and Ben, came swaggering in.

"Greetin's me lads. 'ow be 'ee?" said Ezra. "Will 'ee be joinin' us for supper? Come and sit with us."

Tom's voice trembled as he spoke, "Err… no thank you Ezra, the Captain told us to sit here because Ralph has a job for us."

Ralph stuck his head out of the hatch and called over to the two pirates. "Aye that's right. Leave 'em be, they've got work to do for me." Turning his head towards the boys he said, "Get in 'ere now boys and Isaac will tell 'ee what to do."

The boys heaved a collective sigh of relief. They were delighted Ralph had overheard Tom and backed up his story. They really did not want any involvement with those two characters. Ezra was displeased and it was written all over his face. He stood and walked to the hatch.

"Ye great barrel o' pig's fat. One o' these days I'm goin' to butcher 'ee and cook 'ee in one o'yer own pots! Yer won't 'ave the Cap'n protectin' 'ee fer always."

Ralph just smiled and turned to the boys as they approached him. "Isaac wants 'ee to clean a couple o' them pots over there. Go over there and 'e'll show 'ee what to do."

He gently propelled the boys with his hands over to Isaac who was scrubbing out a pot with an old rag and some sand. He handed over the task to the boys, giving them a wink as he did so.

Turning back, Ralph ladled out some stew to Ezra and Ben, both of them with the ugliest of expressions on their faces.

"This looks like somethin' from the bottom af a pig pen, yer great fat hog! Most likely from yer own pig's hovel. Give me some decent vittles or I'll beat 'ee to a pulp and feed 'ee to the fish."

Ezra was in the mood for some trouble and Tom and Jack guessed that might be because Ralph had protected them. Fear rose inside them as they looked on.

"Ezra, Ben, this all we 'ave, c'mon I'll give 'ee extra rations. All the rest of the crew enjoyed it." Ralph could see what might be coming and was trying to appease them.

Ezra looked down at his plate, "I'll tell 'ee what, you 'ave this slop!"

With that he threw the metal plate of food he was holding at Ralph. It struck him in the face and he reeled back, a cut on his eyebrow already spurting blood from the force of the heavy plate striking him hard. Ezra ran around through the open galley doorway, Ben followed close behind before Ralph could collect himself. Between them they hurled him to the deck. Ezra landed a kick in his Ralph's ribs, yelling, "I'll teach 'ee to interfere with my business."

Ben waded in, the pair of them kicking poor old Ralph who howled with pain as each blow landed. The boys looked on in horror. Isaac darted out of the galley as fast as his limp would allow.

Jack looked around and on his right was a large cast-iron skillet which he picked up in both hands and in one motion brought the heavy pan down on the back of Ezra's head in a fierce forehand blow. Ezra went down as if he'd been shot. Spinning, Jack brought a backhand at Ben, hitting him a glancing blow on the side of his head above his ear. Ben staggered into a table holding his head. Tom kicked him hard in the shin and he yelped not knowing whether to hold his head or his leg. Jack moved in and brought down the pan on the top of Ben's head as he bent towards his shin. He collapsed in a heap on the deck. Ben was also out for the count. The boys bent down over Ralph.

"Are you Okay err… alright Ralph?" enquired Tom.

"I'll be fine if I can get up Jack, I can't thank 'ee boys enough for 'elpin' me out there. I think they might've done for me."

"We couldn't just stand there and let them hurt you Ralph. They're just a pair of vicious bullies. Besides, they attacked you because you protected us in the first place."

They were helping him to his feet as they heard the sound of footsteps rushing down the stairs. It was Ned, leading the way with four hefty-looking members of crew. Isaac had obviously gone for help, which if it hadn't been for the boys may have been too late.

"What's goin' on here me lads? Well I'll be blowed! Look at these two, sleepin' like babies! Who did this?"

"We did sir, they were attacking Ralph for no reason, look at him, he can hardly stand."

"Aye, we can see. Well this is somethin' for the Cap'ns log. Two fierce pirates beaten down by two young boys. Well done lads. The Cap'n will be mighty pleased with 'ee."

"Get these two out of 'ere and clap 'em in irons until the Cap'n decides what to do with 'em."

The four men with Ned strode forward to the fallen bullies and hauled them to their feet and taken off. Their legs were wobbly and they were half dragged, half carried.

Ned looked at the boys. "I think we'll make pirates of 'ee yet lads. That took some courage, I'm impressed. See if 'ee can clean up Ralph's eye there. I'll tell the Cap'n about this and no doubt he'll want to see 'ee. Well done."

At that, Ned left the galley. Jack and Tom knew about first aid, which they'd had to learn in their basic sailing instruction courses. Of course they had no proper medical kit to do the job properly so they did the best they could. They sat Ralph down in a chair and got Isaac to find a clean rag which they used to clean the wound with some water. It wasn't a deep cut and had stopped bleeding. Using another clean rag they put a makeshift bandage around his head to cover the wound. They washed the stew off his face and by the time they had finished, Ralph was smiling again.

"Right boys. Old Ralphie is feeling fine now so I'm going to give 'ee both your suppers."

He went to a large pot which had an iron lid. Having prised it open he took out what looked like a huge joint of beef.

"Pickled beef, me hearties! This is the Capn's but I'm sure 'ee won't mind me givin' 'ee lads some. Anyways, the Cap'n won't know! What 'ee don't know won't 'urt eh?"

At that he launched into raucous laughter as he attacked the beef with a knife, slicing it into thick pieces. After putting it onto plates, he pulled some a boiled yellowish coloured vegetable out of another pan. He finished off the plates with some hardtack biscuits. Ralph obviously thought this was a gourmet meal. He delivered it to the boys as if he were a waiter in a posh restaurant.

"Pickled beef and yam for my brave lads."

Jack and Tom were grateful for Ralph's generosity but not too sure if they were going to enjoy the result of it. The first mouthfuls weren't too bad, the beef was rather sour and the yam was a bit like sweet potato. The hardtack biscuits had tiny insects running around on them. "Weevils," Jack thought.

The boys made all the right noises to please Ralph. "Yum! This is so good. Excellent! Thanks Ralph."

"Well lads, it's a treat for my young friends and defenders, get stuck in there!"

Ralph was rubbing his ribs where he had taken a kicking, he was obviously in some discomfort.

He saw the boys looking at him and said, "I'm fine lads. Just take a bit 'o time. No ribs broken and that's thanks to you lads actin' so quickly. Otherwise I would be in some trouble. Worse though, this ship wouldn't be getting' fed!" More laughter.

They refused second helpings, thanked Ralph, who was gracious once again in his thanks to them for saving him from a beating. The boys said they were tired and going off to their hammocks. When they arrived on their deck, many of the crew were in their hammocks, some were sitting on the deck with their backs against the bulkheads, smoking pipes or just chatting. Several were playing some kind of card game while others looked on. They were gambling, betting with what looked like silver coins. There was the odd shout of triumph when one of them threw down a card. Elsewhere, there was a low murmur of conversation and the odd laugh. Everything stopped as soon as the boys walked in.

"Well, look 'ere, it's our brave young pirates!" someone called out. At that, several of the pirates got to their feet and gathered around Jack and Tom and slapped them on the back.

"Well done lads, 'ee put paid to those two blackguards. They was no good, always causin' a fuss and fights and we believe, murderin' a few 'o the crew they had trouble with. Some men just disappeared overnight, like. No doubt thrown overboard by them rogues! Couldn't be proved though."

The boys revelled in the praise. "Well we had to help old Ralph, he might have been killed," said Jack proudly.

"Aye, just as well 'ee got the better of 'em quickly 'cause old Ezra would 'ave stabbed 'ee without thinkin' 'bout it."

One of the pirates leaned forward looking at the boys earnestly. "Keep away from 'em devils when they is released."

Jack and Tom hadn't even thought of that. They gulped in unison. This led Tom to ask, "What will happen to them? What will their punishment be?"

"Probably fifty lashes at the masthead."

"What? Won't that kill them?" Jack was, in spite of things, horrified.

One of the pirates, smiled and said, "Aye, that it could; and it would be a blessin' but likely they'll be rather poorly for a while."

With a few more pats on the back and "Well done boys."

The pirates returned to their card game or chatting and smoking.

Tom and Jack went to their hammocks and were buzzing with their most recent adventure. "I can't believe we did that, Tom. I just didn't even think about it. When you consider what might have happened if we hadn't knocked them out."

"It doesn't bear thinking about."

"I wonder what new nightmare tomorrow will bring?" Jack heard a soft snore coming from his right. He looked at Tom and he was fast asleep.

Jack closed his eyes and thought of home, his mum and dad and labrador Digby. He followed Tom into sleep, drifting off with those thoughts on his troubled mind.

Four

The next morning they were roused by Ned with the usual racket and ordered, "All hands on deck! All hands on deck!"

The crew made their way up the stairways with groans and moans. Shuffling and stumbling onto the deck they stopped in front of the captain who was on the raised deck above his cabin.

"Mornin' gentlemen." The Captain paused for effect as he gazed around the upturned faces of his crew. After perhaps half a minute, he spoke, "You are 'ere to witness two rogues bein' punished for a crime against a member of this crew. It's not even as if the man they attacked was able to stand up for 'imself. If it weren't for our two newest crew members, young Jack and Tom down there, we would 'ave been without the best ship's cook this side of the ocean. I will not tolerate this sort of behaviour. We need to get along as a crew because we need every man we've got to run this ship and to help plunder the Spanish Main. Every man down means someone else 'as to do their work. When I've finished with these two they won't be able to carry out their duties for some time to come but they 'ave to be punished, so everyone look and learn! Discipline onboard this ship is what I demand!"

He walked down the steps to the deck and everyone, to a man turned to follow the Captain as he walked towards the main mast. There was a commotion as Ned and four hefty pirates dragged a struggling and yelling Ezra and Ben across the deck from below.

"I'm sorry! I'm sorry! It'll never 'appen again." yelled Ezra. His hands were bound in front of him and a rope was around his neck. Two of the men were dragging him by the rope towards the mast.

"Aye, that it won't Master Ezra 'cause if it does, I'll 'ang 'ee from the yard arm. Yer only sorry 'cause 'ee got caught. When this is over stay away from them boys or it will be the worse for 'ee." The Captain was bellowing at Ezra, who was trembling from head to foot. A bully about to get his comeuppance. Ben looked resolute and appeared ready to take his punishment.

"Ned, do yer duty."

The two men dragging Ezra tied him to the mast so his arms were at full stretch above his head. Ned took the collar of Ezra's shirt and ripped the shirt off his back.

"Please! Please! Cap'n, don't do this, I'll do anything, I beg 'ee don't do it!"

Ned had a whip in his hand, the handle was rigid and about two feet long with leather tails about the same length at the end. There were knots at the end of each tail.

The captain gave the ominous command. "Proceed Mr Bosun, fifty lashes."

Ned's arm came flashing around from behind his body. The smack of the leather on bare flesh was like a gunshot. Ezra screamed in pain as the whip split his skin in several places. The boys didn't want to watch but they knew they couldn't walk away. They dropped their heads. Each whiplash brought another scream and more blood. The boys silently counted each stroke. It seemed to take an age. When the fifty lashes were over, they looked at Ezra. He was hanging unconscious, his back a criss-cross of bright red weals and cuts, most of them bleeding.

"Get 'im down Ned and get some salt on his back; and get Ben tied up there." The Captain was stony faced. Ruthless.

Jack and Tom knew about salt being applied to wounds in the old days. It was to help the healing of open wounds but could only guess that it would make the pain ten times worse.

Ezra was dragged across the deck, laid down and Ralph applied a layer of salt to his back from a wooden bucket. The unconscious pirate awoke screaming. The open wounds were stinging with the salt, he was in agony with more pain than he had experienced in all of his life. Ralph gave a malicious little smile at the irony of the situation, pleased to be getting his revenge.

Ben was next, tied up to the mast and after the Captain gave the order for Ned to start the punishment, he didn't scream, he made grunting noises like an animal and tugged at his bindings, stiffening his body with the pain at each lash. He suffered his punishment and was conscious all the way through. He too had his wounds salted and along with Ezra was half dragged, half carried below decks to their hammocks where they were unceremoniously dumped.

Jack and Tom felt physically sick. They had never witnessed such brutality in their young lives. The thought of a coming sea battle and seeing people killing each other was absolutely terrifying. They were going to have to toughen up. They had no idea how long this nightmare was going to continue.

The crew started to disperse back to their duties. Jack said, "Come on Tom. Back to work."

They headed back to the armoury where Jasper was already there, unlocking the door. He had sneaked below before Ben was lashed, he had seen enough with Ezra.

"What did you think of that, boys?" Jasper's face was white and he looked so shocked.

"Horrible!" The boys spoke as one.

"I suppose there has to be discipline, and brutes like those two should never expect to get away with that sort of behaviour. Old Ralph is a decent man and wouldn't hurt a fly. If you two hadn't intervened they might have killed him. But still, it's just so shocking to watch."

Tom and Jack nodded in agreement. They settled down on barrels and started the tedious job of filling the packets with gunpowder.

"What if we underfilled these packets so the guns didn't fire as far? We wouldn't be killing as many Spaniards." Tom's face was lit up with what he thought was a brilliant idea.

Jasper grinned but without any humour, said, "Well Tom, first, I dare say the gunners would notice and even if they didn't, we would be putting ourselves in danger because we wouldn't be able to defend ourselves when the Spaniards fight back, because they won't have under-powered guns, that's for sure. And second, how good is your Spanish? Maybe you could tell them that you are from another century and shouldn't be here."

"Oh, right! Didn't think of that." Tom kept his head down, embarrassed at his silly suggestion. "Well, it's just a thought."

Jack didn't comment because it was futile, they were here, had to do as they were told and get on with it.

The three boys worked on. The heat inside the ship was almost unbearable, the tropical sun and humidity made life so much harder. By mid-day they had made and distributed to the guns so many packets they had lost count. They stopped briefly for some food and water and afterwards, carried on through until sunset.

Just as they were packing up for the night, Ralph appeared with a small pot of stew, some bread, plates and a bowl with some large yellowish egg-shaped fruits. I thought I would bring yer grub to 'ee boys bein' as I brought 'ee a treat. From the bowl he lifted out three strange bruised-looking fruits and gave one each to the boys.

"Look 'ere, get a knife and peel the skin off, these is what the Spaniards call papaya. They be delicious. Get 'em down 'ee before anyone else sees 'em."

Jack and Tom had eaten papayas before, as their mothers got them occasionally in local supermarkets but they didn't let on to Ralph. The boys took a knife each, skinned the fruit and quickly wolfed them down. They were delicious and it was so good to get some decent food inside them. Strangely, the boys thought nothing of eating "dessert" before the main course. Ralph left them to it. They attacked the stew with relish and when they had finished, they took back their plates and bowls, thanked Ralph and went to the sleeping quarters.

As they walked in, several of the pirates called out their names, "Jack! Tom! 'ow be 'ee lads?" Various congratulations were called out to them, even though they'd had a similar welcome the previous evening. It appeared that Ezra and Ben were feared by many of the crew and were delighted to see them lashed.

They were picking up the names of some of the crew and they called back, "Fine thanks, Jim, Alf, Pedro, how are you gentlemen?"

"Ooohh! Gentlemen is we?" called back Jim. "Well kind sirs, we be just fine an'all."

The banter went back and forwards, mostly from the crew who were enjoying themselves, teasing the boys.

"I expects 'ee will be the Cap'ns best friends now, eh lads? Yer bravery knows no bounds!" Gales of laughter followed. "We'll be needing brave young fellers like 'ee when we meets our next Spaniard! Every one of the crew 'as to play 'is part. Ask the Cap'n fer a cutlass or at least a dagger each."

Jack and Tom looked at each other, eyes wide. It hadn't dawned on them that they might have to fight, when and if they met a Spanish ship.

Jack lowered his voice, "My goodness Tom, do you think they're serious?"

"I'm not sure if they're teasing us, we should ask Ralph tomorrow. He'll tell us. I sincerely hope they were teasing us!"

The boys climbed into their hammocks like seasoned old sailors. They both lay awake for a while again, thinking about home, their families and how they just had to escape. Too tired from their exertions to chat, they fell asleep.

***

Roused from sleep by Ned, who never seemed to rest, they turned out and went for breakfast, Ralph made them wait till last again and gave them some sort of gruel or oatmeal porridge with cane sugar on it, which was not too bad and filled them up. They exchanged some banter with some of the pirates who were beginning to treat them like part of the crew after their adventure with Ezra and Ben.

When an opportunity arose, Tom went up to Ralph and asked him if they were going to have to fight when they attacked a Spanish ship.

"Nay lad. But I will see if I can get the Cap'n to give 'ee a dagger or knife each to protect yerselves with. Them crewmates was just havin' fun with 'ee."

The boys heaved a collective sigh of relief, leaving the galley and trudging off to the armoury. Jasper was there already, sorting out the powder bags ready for Jack and Tom to start making up the packets.

"Jack, Tom, good morning to you. How goes it?"

"Hello Jasper," replied Jack. "It's okay, it seems as if we are becoming accepted by the crew after the Ezra and Ned incident."

Jasper responded sharply, "I'm sure you are. But be careful, this is a bunch of wicked cut-throats who would sell you as slaves as soon as look at you. Thinking you are friendly with these men is an illusion. They don't care about anyone but themselves."

Jasper was bitter and had every right to be, he and his sister having been kidnapped. Plus the fact that their father had paid a large ransom and they hadn't been released.

"Well Jasper, I think we would rather appear to be on friendly terms than not," said Tom. "It might help us somewhere in the future. We're in the same situation as you and Kate. Although we've got families who don't even know where we are."

Jasper smiled, "Yes I know. I do get depressed by the whole thing. It weighs me down sometimes. I'm sorry, I didn't mean to be short with you."

"OK," said Jack, "let's get working here and make sure we've got enough powder packets to make sure we win any gun battles we might have."

The boys set to and were becoming very adept at the job. The packets started piling up and had to be taken to the guns. They toiled all morning and after a mid-day break carried on throughout the afternoon. By sunset their bodies were aching with weariness, carrying the powder packets to the guns was an exhausting chore. Evening meal came and went and just as the boys were heading for their hammocks, Ned appeared and told them the Captain wanted to see them. Hearts in mouths they proceeded to Edward Boyle's cabin.

"Come in lads," boomed the captain, "pull up a chair." Once again, the boys had to use all their strength to move the massive oak chairs.

"Well lads, just a day or two till we sees some action," Boyle narrowed his eyes and his grin made Jack and Tom shrink inside. "Tom, my lad, tell me now the exact position and time where we will get sight of the Spaniard?"

Tom felt sick, he got out his mobile phone, hands trembling and did some make believe calculations. Looking at the Captain, he stammered, "Errr… mid afternoon, sir and just where we said it would be the other day when we were looking at your chart."

"Give me that thing," the Captain snapped as he held out his hand for the phone. Tom placed it into his hand, gulping hard as he did.

The Captain turned in his chair and threw the phone through the open window. As he did he guffawed with laughter. Looking at the boys his face was lit up with humour.

"Come now boys, you didn't think old Ed Boyle was as stupid as that did 'ee? I've teased you all along, pretendin' to believe all that nonsense about a magic box."

He bellowed with laughter again, then smiling, said, "It's alright. I would have done the same if I'd been in your boots. Yer was just tryin' to win some favour with old Edward 'ere. We'll find a Spaniard I'm certain of it, but it's with my clever intuition." Boyle said the word like intooishun. "I doesn't need no magic box. I'm a clever tactition. Look, I've talked to Ned and Ralph and they both think yer good lads. 'ard workers and brave too, the way 'ee dealt with those two ruffians who attacked Ralph. Go that cabinet behind 'ee and choose a knife each and stick it yer belt. 'ee might need it. There's plenty of 'em what we've taken from some o' them Spanish." He was grinning from ear to ear enjoying the boys' embarrassment.

The boys stood, relieved the silly ordeal that Tom had talked them into, was over.

"Thank you Captain," Tom was grinning sheepishly.

"Yes, thank you sir," said Jack. "Err, when we attack the Spanish ship, where do you want us to be?"

"Lock yerselves in the armoury and don't let anyone in there. Stab 'em if necessary and that includes our own men."

"Yes sir." Jack and Tom exchanged terrified glances as they turned and opened the cabinet doors. On the lower shelf was an array of about twenty wicked-looking knives and daggers. The boys chose one each. Similar in size with wooden handles and black steel blades about eight inches long.

They thanked Captain Boyle again and left. He said nothing and didn't even look up from his chart.

"We can thank our lucky stars Tom. Thank goodness that's over with. I thought we were going to be tied to the mast and lashed." Relief was all over Jack's face.

"Yes, I know but my Dad will go mad that I've lost my phone. I can't tell him a pirate Captain threw it in the sea, can I? Who would believe that?"

"Look Tom, there are two things here. First, a lost phone is better than a lashing and second, we have to get home first before we can tell your Dad anything!"

"I suppose so."

Five

The next two days were routine, more gunpowder packets, more of Ralph's concoctions and more ribbing and teasing by the crew. Ezra and Ben had not been able to get out of their hammocks or get food and drink without help. On two occasions Jack and Tom had been ordered to take them water. On the first occasion, Ezra had looked at Jack and said in a hiss, "I will get 'ee lad. I'll cut yer throat if it's the last thing I does."

Jack felt a chill run right through him but a strange defiance welled up inside. He pulled out the knife the Captain had given him, held it in front of Ezra's face and said, "Not if I cut yours first, you bully!"

Ezra's eyes widened and he fell back into his hammock, saying nothing.

"I can't believe you just said that Jack!" Tom was incredulous.

"Nor can I. My knees have gone weak." Jack was pleased with himself but wasn't deluded enough to want to be around when Ezra recovered.

***

The days were long, tedious and hard, the only respite being meal times and conversations with Jasper. Finishing for the day, they ate their evening meal, being cheered up a little by Ralph's seemingly unlimited good humour, they climbed into their hammocks. They were continually exhausted.

The next day, the boys awoke to the usual barking command from Ned. As their feet touched the floor, they heard cries from above. Loud, urgent yells. Ned turned and ran up the stairs to the main deck. The crew members who had moments before been sleeping in their hammocks leapt out and began running to their posts.

"What's going on?" Jack shouted to at the closest pirate who was dashing past.

"It's a Spaniard, lad. Better get to yer post!"

Fear coursed through Jack and Tom. This was it. They had hoped it would not happen, but here it was. They were looking at the possibility of a violent death. They picked up their knives and holding them at their sides ran to the armoury. Jasper was just arriving there with Kate.

"Jack, Tom, come in and lock the gate behind you, pull out the keys." Jasper had a musket which was almost as tall as the boys. "This will keep us safe if any of the Spaniards get down here."

Jack and Tom were not reassured. One musket against a ship load of Spaniards? The odds didn't sound too good.

"Gentlemen, this is Kate my sister. Kate, this is Jack Andrews and Tom Williams." Jasper made the introductions.

Both boys shook Kate's hand and said, "Pleased to meet you." Tom added, "But I wish we had met in better circumstances."

Kate was a pretty girl, tall for her age with long brown hair. She smiled and agreed with Tom.

"Why is Kate here Jasper?" asked Tom.

"Last action, a cannonball hit the area above her cabin. She suffered no injury but I convinced Captain Boyle to let me bring her down here in the centre of the ship where I hope we will all be safer. She is after all, worth ransom money to him, so he agreed."

Time stood still for the occupants of the armoury. They knew they had to keep producing the powder packets to replace those which were going to be used in the fight but fear gnawed at them. They were terrified.

"Come on boys, let's keep busy, it will help." Jasper started filling some bags with powder. Jack and Tom joined in.

They could hear feet running around the gun decks above them, muffled shouts came through the planking decks. The voices and shouting abated, they were sailing towards a fight and the crew were ready for it. Suddenly, they felt the ship heave into what was a severe change of direction.

"What's going on Jasper?" Tom's face was riven with terror.

"We've swung broadside on to give them a volley of cannon fire."

At that, there was a series of explosions from the port side that rocked the ship. The noise was deafening. The battle had started. They could hear the massive cannons made from cast iron, which weighed tons, rolling across the deck above with the recoil of the shot. The gunners were shouting out commands. Jack and Tom felt the atmosphere, it was electric; they could also smell the gunpowder fumes as they drifted down to their deck. After what seemed an age but was probably only a few minutes, they felt the ship change direction again.

"We've swung back on a forward heading to present a smaller target with only the bows facing them. We must have caused them some damage because we haven't fired for a few minutes now," explained Jasper.

The words were no sooner out of his mouth when the ship gave a massive shudder and lurched in the water. They had been hit, somewhere at the front. They could hear cannonballs screaming past.

"Well that didn't work!" yelled Tom over the increasing noise. "Turning front on still gave them a big enough target!"

Jasper shouted back, "Just imagine what might have happened if we had been side on. All those cannonballs that missed us would probably have hit!"

As he spoke the ship turned and moments later fired another broadside. They heard the gunners above cheer.

"That must have been an effective broadside," said Jasper.

Within a few minutes another broadside thundered out, rocking the ship. The noise of the massive guns rolling across the deck above sounded like trains going over a railway bridge to Jack. Another cheer from above although giving the boys some confidence in terms of their own survival, they shuddered to think about the people on board the Spanish ship. There was momentary silence and the Captain's booming voice could be heard from three decks above.

"Prepare to board! Grappling hooks to the ready! Swivel gunners, fire and reload at will till I tell 'ee to stop!"

The boys' hearts almost stopped. The pirate crew was about to board the Spanish ship. "What are the swivel guns, Jasper?"

"They're small bore guns mounted on the ship's rails for firing grapeshot to kill as many Spaniards as possible before boarding!" Jasper's voice had a strong emotional quality to it. Fear made it wobble.

The loud crack of these weapons resonated through the ship. The cacophony of noise started up again and after what seemed an age, they heard the Captain's voice screaming, "Cease fire!" to the swivel gunners.

The ship shuddered as it crashed sideways into the Spanish galleon. More yelling and shouting came from above along with the sound of steel striking steel where cutlasses were being slashed against Spanish swords. Volleys of musket shots could be heard. The battle for survival and victory was well and truly underway on the decks above. Jasper and the boys hadn't filled a powder bag in the past half hour. Fear had turned them into statues. Not knowing what was going on was the worst.

As time went on the noise started to reduce. Less shouting and yelling, less musket shots and and the clash of sword upon sword. After what seemed a lifetime later, they heard footsteps rushing down the stairs. It was Ned.

"Come out of there you lads and get on deck. The Spaniards have a company of soldiers on board. We're fighting for our lives, we've lost most of the crew! Come on hurry up!"

Jasper unlocked the barred gate and the boys stepped out in a daze, fear coursing through their bodies almost wetting themselves. Jasper locked the gate with Kate still in the armoury, leaving her with the musket. She was distraught and crying. Jasper spoke up.

"Please Ned, they're just young boys they can't fight soldiers!"

"Even old Ralph and Isaac are on deck doin' their bit. Come on hurry, get up there, when you get on deck, pick up a cutlass and defend this ship!"

Jack and Tom could barely move one foot in front of another such was their terror. They climbed the stairs and stopped at the door at the top of the stairs surveying the scene on deck. The main deck was manic. The ships were side by side pulled together by the grappling hooks the pirates had used. Spanish soldiers in full armour were swarming all over the Pelican's deck, some firing muskets and others slashing swords at the remaining pirate crew. Bleeding bodies littered the deck, screams and yells filled the air. Tom spotted Ralph sitting on the deck, his back against the bulwark with blood pouring from his shoulder. Isaac lay face down and not moving.

"Look over there Jack! It's Ralph and he's wounded. Let's help him!"

Jack's gaze followed Tom's pointing finger and spotted Ralph. Adrenaline was coursing round their veins. They dashed from the doorway, Jack stooped and picked up a sword from the deck, Tom got himself up a curved cutlass which had blood smeared up the blade. Such was their terror, their legs felt as if they wouldn't bear their weight. They reached Ralph and dropped to their knees to look at his wound which was in his shoulder, it was deep and bleeding profusely.

"Ralph!" cried Jack. "What have you been doing? Let's get you off this deck. A chap your age shouldn't be up here fighting." Neither should we, he thought to himself.

"Look behind 'ee lads, Spaniard!" Ralph screamed out.

Jack and Tom turned to see a Spanish soldier rushing across the deck at them, sword outstretched in front of him. In a split second Jack leapt forward and dropped to his hands and knees, back parallel to the deck. Caught entirely by surprise, the onrushing Spaniard's legs crashed into Jack's crouched body and he tripped. He rocketed onto the edge of the bulwark head first, overhanging the sea. Tom, quick as a flash grabbed his feet and gave a heave and helped the armour-laden soldier on his way. A scream of terror emitted from his mouth as he hurtled towards the sea. A huge splash followed and he disappeared into the depths. Tom was horrified what they had just done.

Jack instinctively aware what was going through Tom's mind, shouted, "Come on Tom, it was him or us!"

The fighting continued around them as they dragged the injured Ralph to one of the forward cabins. Inside they shut the doors and together dragged a large cupboard across them, hoping this would keep out the Spaniards. Looking inside the cupboard, Tom found a linen shirt which he began to tear into strips. Jack quickly got the idea of what he was doing and took a large piece and made it into a pad which he put on the wound. Tom used the other strips and bound the pad in place as tightly as he could. Ralph gasped in pain.

"Sorry Ralph but we've got to stop the bleeding," said Tom.

"I know lad, and I'm grateful to 'ee. Thanks for 'elpin' me. At least I'm alive." He paused, then added, "At the moment, anyway." He chuckled, then looked serious. "Poor old Isaac 'as joined 'is ancestors." A tear rolled down his cheek.

"What happened here Ralph? Why did it go so badly?" asked Tom.

"It was a trap. They took a big risk as we could have destroyed 'em with cannonfire but I reckon they 'ad 'eard about Cap'n Boyle's tactics and expected a quick assault then a boarding to take over the ship. We thought we 'ad 'em when we outgunned 'em. Blew their mizzen mast right off the deck, shattered the captain's cabin and almost destroyed their starboard gun ports. They couldn't turn quickly when we took off their mast, so we thought we'd got 'em where we wanted 'em. As we pulled 'em in on the grapplin' 'ooks a company of soldiers poured from below decks. We couldn't cope with such numbers, well armed and in full armour. We was doomed."

The noise from outside had almost ceased. Suddenly, the cabin doors burst inwards, the cupboard tipping over crashing to the floor. It was Captain Boyle. A huge stain of blood covered from high on his chest to half way down his front. He could barely stand. Even so, his massive bulk and strength had allowed him to force the doors and tip over the cupboard. He dropped to his knees and smiled an awful smile. The boys were transfixed, couldn't speak, couldn't move.

"They must've 'ad over an 'undred Spanish soldiers on board, ready for us! We couldn't handle 'em. They was just too many."

Edward Boyle suddenly pitched forward, crashing onto the floor and breathed his last. The three of them looked at each other in dismay. This wasn't what they had expected. They were now at the mercy of the Spanish victors. Jack and Tom felt sick. Before this, not only had they not seen a dead body before but neither had they seen anyone die, now they had seen too many. The savagery of the violence they had seen was shocking.

"What are we going to do?" Jack's voice went up an octave.

The words weren't out of his mouth when crunching footsteps could be heard on the deck. A contingent of five Spanish soldiers ran into the cabin, four of them with their muskets at the ready. The onc at the front held a double edged sword with an inch wide blade which tapered to a sharp point.

They were in full armour with the unmistakeable steel helmets, so familiar were they, that Jack and Tom could have drawn a picture had they been asked to do so. Behind the main group the boys caught a glimpse of Jasper and Kate. Two soldiers were holding them.

A torrent of Spanish came out of the mouth of the leading soldier who appeared to be in charge. The soldiers who were at the side of Jasper and Kate brought the brother and sister to where Jack and Tom were. The leader smiled and spoke in a quieter voice and turned back toward the deck.

"Sigame, por favor."

They could only assume this meant follow or come with me, so they followed. Jasper and Kate behind Jack and Tom as they followed the Spaniard. The group of soldiers brought up the rear. The sight that greeted them was like a film set of a battle, except this was real. The smell of gunpowder assailed their nostrils. There were dead bodies and wounded pirates and Spaniards everywhere. The moaning and screaming of the injured was horrifying. They were brought to the raised deck at the front of The Pelican and climbed the steps to where a rather grand-looking gentleman stood. He was dressed in a white shirt with very baggy sleeves done up at the wrists and long black leather boots up beyond his knees to thigh height. A broad black belt went from his right shoulder to his left hip from which was hanging a sword in its scabbard which looked as if it had a real silver handguard. He had long dark hair and a beard and moustache, he looked like the paintings of the English King, Charles I, Jack and Tom had seen in books and on television.

"Lady and gentlemen, I am El Conde Fernan Gonzalez, perhaps you would be good enough to tell me who you are and why a girl so young is on board a pirate ship?" He pronounced ship as 'sheep' but his English seemed flawless otherwise.

Jasper stepped forward and introduced Kate, then Jack and Tom and explained the circumstances of their presence.

El Conde shook hands with the boys and kissed the back of Kate's hand. She blushed bright red. He asked a number of questions about their capture and what they were made to do whilst on board The Pelican and how they were treated. Jasper went through his story quickly. He explained why they were onboard the Pelican and that they had been kidnapped and held to ransom, that their father was in Jamaica and who he was.

Tom told a version of their story which was an outrageous lie, as he didn't want to go into their actual tale of woe. He told El Conde that they were cousins and they had been on a visit to their uncle in Antigua from their home in Cornwall England, and had been kidnapped when they were fishing in a small boat. Jack's head snapped round at Tom, he was doing it again, just like he did with his phone. Tom chose Antigua at random as he couldn't think of the name of another Caribbean island. It was rather a weak story but El Conde didn't seem to care as he asked them nothing else, he just uttered the word, "Cornwall," almost to himself, as if he were confirming what they had said.

El Conde smiled and said, "Well my young friends, you will be pleased that we have rescued you from the clutches of those terrible pirates. I regret you have been involved in such awful carnage but I will ensure your safety and make sure you are returned to your families as soon as possible. Spain and England are at peace after many years at war and we will have to go to Jamaica for repairs. The English have very good facilities for such things but they will make us pay heavily for the privilege."

In spite of what had happened and with dead and dying all around them, Kate and the boys couldn't help producing a little grin. They were going home.

"Thank you sir, thank you," they spoke in unison.

"First, however, we must make this vessel seaworthy, I will get my carpenters working on the damage to the bow. Fortunately, there is little damage to The Pelican, unlike our own ship, The San Francisco, which suffered at the hands of the very efficient pirate gunners. We will be transferring my crew to this ship and towing our own back to Jamaica for repairs. I will leave you in the hands of my second-in-command, Pablo Veraz who will take you to the deceased pirate Captain's cabin." He turned to a young man, also dressed like a nobleman. "Pablo, por favor."

They were escorted to Captain Boyle's cabin by Pablo. The Spanish ship, The San Francisco, was alongside and showing the effects of the cannonfire. The main central mast was completely destroyed and lying half across the deck and hanging over the water. There were huge chunks of the bulwark missing where the cannonballs had ploughed through the thick timbers. The bodies of the pirates, the Spanish crew and soldiers strewn around the decks of both ships made for an horrific sight. Jack and Tom felt as if they were dreaming or stuck in a video game.

On reaching the cabin, they were told politely to remain in there. Pablo bowed and left, closing the door. Once on their own they sat at the Captain's table and spoke excitedly of the prospects of being released. Jasper seemed quiet and made the point that he would believe it when he and Kate were with their father.

"Come on Jasper," said Tom. "El Conde seems like a decent man. I'm sure he's genuine. By the way, what's an El Conde?"

"I believe it's a nobleman, in English I think we would call him a Count."

"They were obviously more than prepared for an attack by a pirate ship carrying many soldiers on board," Jack said.

"I suppose depending on what they carrying they might decide to give themselves more protection. This Spanish ship might be carrying a very valuable cargo bound for Spain," responded Jasper.

"Or maybe they were they were just fed up being attacked and wanted to end Edward Boyle's plundering in the Caribbean," ventured Jack.

Tom pointed at the wooden chests against the outer wall of the cabin. "Just look in those chests and you will see that Jack is most likely right. That's probably Spanish treasure, stolen by the pirates. They've got it back now."

Jasper stood and walked over to the chests and opened one lid after another, looking in, he gasped at the gold treasures almost overflowing the chest. Kate looking over from the table, shook her head in awe. Jasper sat down again and as they were discussing their freedom and how they might get home, they heard footsteps descending the stairs to the cabin. The door opened and El Conde entered, grinning widely.

"Lady and gentlemen, as I explained we have to sail to Jamaica, because that is closest for the best repairs and especially as we have to tow our ship. We will have the seaworthiness of the San Francisco assessed and conduct necessary repairs. We will ensure Jasper and Kate get back to their family home and then when we are repaired, we will cross the Atlantic to Spain. As I said, Spain and England have recently finished a long war but even so, we will take a huge risk and put Jack and Tom ashore in the West of England. You will be pleased, yes?"

Jack and Tom's faces were full of panic.

"Err, sir, we err need to get back to Antigua to our uncle so he knows we are safe." Tom's voice had a pleading ring to it.

"Nonsense, we will get a message to your uncle to tell him you are safe and are being taken back to England." He had decided and changed the subject, "I have arranged for you to have some food."

The boys thought at this stage that it was probably futile to argue.

"Excuse me sir," Jasper spoke up. "What will happen to Ralph, he's the ship's cook who was the wounded man in the cabin Jack and Tom were in?"

"Oh, yes, the old man. He will be imprisoned with the remaining pirates on the San Francisco and on our return to Spain, he will be tried by a legal court for piracy."

At that El Conde turned on his heel and left the cabin. Jack and Tom felt very sad about Ralph who had been nothing but kind to them. Equally, they were horrified that they were going to be taken back to England with the date 1720, they would never get home, they needed to get back to the cave that brought them to this place and this century.

"What's in this for El Conde to take us to England? It doesn't make sense." Jack shook his head in dismay.

Tom spoke up, "Well, it seems he is set on it so we need to escape before we set sail across the Atlantic, Jasper. I know it's difficult and seems preposterous but we are from the future and the only way back home is through the cave that got us here."

"I do not know about El Conde's reasons, and have no understanding of what you mean and how you got here from the future, but I believe you. When they release Kate and me, we will see if we can get you ashore in Jamaica and help you escape. I am sure my Father will help."

"Thank you Jasper, this really is a terrifying situation for us but I suppose less terrifying than being in the hands of the pirates."

They could hear shouting and movement as feet crashed around on deck above. Hearing some splashes from the sea they looked out of the window and saw bodies hurtling into the water. Jack and Tom just looked at each other and shrugged. They had to steel themselves and didn't think they would get used to death. This was, for the Spanish, just a clearing up exercise. Tom and Jack knew that nothing else could be done with the bodies.

The main part of the Spanish crew transferred to The Pelican and it took most of the rest of the day for their carpenters to repair the damage to the bow. When they were ready, well into the evening, they set sail and the Spanish ship was manned with a skeleton crew and towed behind The Pelican. All the dead bodies of the pirates had been thrown overboard without ceremony. The Spanish dead had been given quick religious funerals but also dropped into a watery grave. Such was life at sea in the early eighteenth century.

Jasper and Kate, Jack and Tom were still in the Captain's cabin when they set sail and after what seemed an age a Spanish sailor entered the cabin and wordlessly set down a large tray with a pile of sliced cured ham, cooked potatoes and what looked like dried tomatoes. In a bowl were four bananas.

A large flagon of water stood on the tray. It seemed evident that the Spaniards had a much better idea of how to eat than a bunch of wild pirates and of course they had only left port that morning fully loaded with fresh provisions for a long trip.

The four tucked in, the excitement and terror of the day had used up so much adrenaline they were both starving and very tired. There was a silence between them as the thoughts of Jasper and Kate lingered on seeing their families. Jack and Tom, however, were highly concerned that they were going to end up in Cornwall in the wrong century.

Kate spoke suddenly, breaking the silence. "Listen, Tom and Jack. I think I should try and persuade El Conde that you should come back to my father's home and tell them that he will get you back to Cornwall on one his ships taking sugar back to England. I'm sure he might agree. What do you think?"

"Do you think he will agree? It's worth a try Kate, he might listen to you, I've noticed how sort of, err… extra polite he is with you."

Jasper responded, "Good idea Kate, we have nothing to lose in trying. Let us see if we can get some sleep and wait to speak to El Conde in the morning."

"We appreciate your help, this is a desperate situation for us," Tom's anxiety was evident as he spoke.

"We'll do what we can."

After their meal, the four teenagers split up. Jasper went find Pablo Veraz and got permission for he and Kate to sleep in the cabin where Kate had been held prisoner. Jack and Tom climbed into Captain Boyle's bunk, deciding to share the relatively narrow, rather hard mattress. They were asleep in seconds.

The boys awoke to see daylight outside the cabin window. Standing up they felt as if they had been hit by a truck, so sore and stiff were their muscles.

"We're still on the way to Jamaica, presumably."

Jack looking out of the window could see they were still sailing, carried by what appeared to be a good breeze, with white caps on the waves. The Spanish ship was only about a hundred feet or so from the stern of The Pelican, being towed along. "Yesterday seems like a bad dream," uttered Tom. "I suppose we're lucky to be alive. Let's hope we can get back to the cave and get home."

They climbed the stairs up to the deck. Standing there, El Conde greeted them with a bow and a greeting. "Buenas dias, muchachos, how are you? Did you sleep well?" His English was accented but excellent. Tom and Jack had seen enough Spaniards and Mexicans in films to know what Buenas Dias meant.

"Good morning," the boys replied, almost in unison. "Yes thank you," said Jack.

"Would you like to eat some food?"

"Yes, sir," Tom spoke for both of them. "Thank you."

"I'm hungry," said Jack.

"Then you must follow Miguel," El Conde signalled to a short, muscular-looking deckhand and spoke in rapid spanish, "Miguel will take you to the galley and arrange for you to eat."

"Thank you very much, sir."

They fell in behind Miguel and made their way down to The Pelican's galley. As they entered, the aroma coming from the cooking pots assailed their nostrils. They picked up a wooden bowl each at the side of the serving hatch and held them out in front of the cook, a Spaniard who had taken over Ralph's kitchen and was as unsmiling as Ralph was cheerful. He just stared at them. Miguel issued what sounded like a command with the only words they understood in the sentence, "El Conde" and the cook ladled what looked like a stew into their bowls. Taking wooden spoons from a box they sat at a table and tried the stew. It was delicious, with what looked and tasted like a spicy sausage with white beans. They made short work of it and went back to the serving hatch. They were expending so much energy with stress, it seemed as if they couldn't get enough grub.

Jack mustered one of his only Spanish phrases, "Por favor?" He felt like Oliver Twist asking for more. He held his breath. The cook grimaced, didn't seem to be happy and muttered under his breath but he ladled more stew into their bowls. Sitting again, they had just about to started to discuss how they might escape if El Conde was dead set on taking them to England, when Kate and Jasper came in, again led by Miguel. There were no queries or sour questioning looks from the cook; they were served with food and came over and sat opposite Jack and Tom.

Kate didn't look too happy. "What's the matter Kate?" enquired Tom. Are you still upset by yesterday's battle?

"No Tom, I asked El Conde if you could come with us to our father's home and he said no. He wanted to take you to England because he wanted to show the English that Spain had rescued you from evil pirates. I think he wants to show off and look good to the English authorities and hopes it will get back to his King."

Boys felt the panic rise. This really was awful. They envisaged their lives in eighteenth century England, no parents, no family. What on earth were they going to do?

"We have got to get off this ship when we get to port." Tom's voice was strident and emotional.

Close to tears, Jack agreed. "I think we've got to get over the side and swim before the ship actually docks," said Jack. "If they see us, I don't think they will shoot us or anything. What do you all think?"

Jasper spoke up. "I asked El Conde when we would arrive in Jamaica, and he said, depending on the wind and tide, it was likely to be after dark tomorrow night. Towing their damaged ship is slowing us down. I think your best opportunity is going to be after dark to slip into the water and swim ashore."

"Yes!" hissed Jack, he felt optimistic for the first time in days.

Tom was nodding his head vigorously. He too was smiling. "Not a very sophisticated plan but it does give us some hope." His smile disappeared as quickly as it came. He had just had a worrying thought. "What do we do once ashore. How do we get to your father's home?"

Kate interjected, "We will draw you a map of how to get to our father's house. It's only a few miles from the port where we will dock. Father will help you, I know he will."

"Fantastic!" Tom was feeling better with just those few words. "OK, let's hope we do get there in the dark."

The rest of the day dragged. They ate well and were treated courteously, went to bed and started the seemingly interminable wait again the next morning.

After breakfast, the four of them walked the decks endlessly, looking out to sea, wondering when they might see land ahead of them. They ate another meal in the middle of the day, it was the same as breakfast. Tom and Jack agreed that they would never be fussy over food again. Anything would be better than some of the food they'd had since becoming caught up in this terrifying situation.

In mid afternoon, a shout came from the crow's nest. It became obvious that another ship had been seen sailing towards them. The boy's hearts sank. Please no more fighting, thought Jack. The others were thinking the same thing. For a few minutes the crew stood to their battle positions until they were told to relax by their superior officers. It was a Spanish ship. The orders were given to haul up the sails and stop the Pelican. The anchor of the San Francisco, being towed behind, was dropped so the two ships didn't crash together.

They slowed to a halt about fifty yards from the other ship, which had also been brought to a stop. A longboat was lowered from the other ship, which they could now see was called "Santa Anna". The boat made its way towards the Pelican. It came alongside and two men who were rather fancily dressed like El Conde, climbed up the side and came aboard. They were probably some kind of officers. There was much hand shaking, laughing and back slapping between the visitors and El Conde and Pablo Veraz. It looked like they all knew each other. In the course of conversation, Pablo went down below decks and came back holding a scroll of paper or parchment, they couldn't tell, which was rolled and sealed with red wax and a ribbon. He passed this to one of the men from the Santa Anna.

Orders were shouted and about a dozen members of crew started to head down the stairs to where Edward Boyle's cabin was. After a few minutes, back they came, struggling up the stairs carrying what the youngsters knew were the chests full of treasure, four men carrying each. One of these was lowered into the rowing boat by a pulley attached to a jib which swung out from the forward mast. In quite a laborious, time consuming operation, the rowing boat ferried back and forth three times, taking a treasure chest on each journey.

When the transfer of the treasure was completed, the visitors left, climbed down into their longboat and were rowed back to their ship. The Pelican soon set sail again and was pushed along by a stiff breeze. White caps spilled off the top of small waves.

El Conde approached the three boys and Kate. "That was my good friend Don Esteban Jiminez, Captain of the Santa Anna. He is on his way to Spain. I took the opportunity to give him a letter for our King Philip, describing our adventures of the past few days and as you may have deduced, he is returning stolen Spanish treasure to our country. His Majesty will be very pleased with me for destroying one of the scourges of Spanish ships, the dreadful, murderous pirate, Edward Boyle. And you know children, you will be famous in Spain because I have mentioned you too. I have told His Majesty that I am taking you, Tom and Jack, back to England. Is that not good?"

Very pleased with himself, El Conde turned and went down to his cabin. The boys didn't think it was very good at all. In fact, it was very bad.

Jasper went below deck for about fifteen minutes and came back with a scrap of rough paper which he passed surreptitiously to Jack. It was a map drawn in ink. The boys glanced at it and not wanting to be seen with it, Jack slid it into his pocket and said, "Thank you so much Jasper. What's the name of your father's estate? It makes sense to know because this map might be useless after we get out of the water."

"As you know, our name is Bennett, our father is Sir James Bennett and his estate is called Old Sussex Hall. It's on the main road west from Port Royal. Even if you lose the map, it's easy to find. To the west of the town is a large hill named Spy Glass Hill. If you get past it or over it you cannot miss Old Sussex Hall, it's rather large." The boys smiled, new found hope filled them. They couldn't wait till dark.

The day passed slowly and their anxiety was high, however, they were glad that land was not yet in sight. They wanted a night-time arrival. Eventually, the sun started dropping in the western sky and the light dimmed as dusk crept upon them. A cry came from the crow's nest and the deck hands ran to the sides of the ship and looked in the direction of travel. The four youngsters rushed to look too. They could see twinkling lights, getting brighter as the it got darker. The dark mass of mountains of Jamaica stood out as the sun's last rays silhouetted them.

The lights got steadily closer. They could see a small sailing boat coming towards them. There was much industry on board as The Pelican edged towards the island. Those in charge yelled orders, the crew ran to and fro, hauling up some of the sails and generally carrying out whatever they needed to do to dock the ships. Four large rowing boats were lowered, two from The Pelican and two from San Francisco and each was manned by an eight-man crew with a tillerman at the back to steer. The tow rope between the ships was released. Crew members from each of the ships threw ropes to each of the rowing boats to where they were attached. The rowers began their back breaking task of towing in the creaking and undulating ships. As they approached within a few hundred yards of port, the rest of the sails were hauled up and The Pelican slowed quickly.

It was obvious that these large ships had to be towed into the dock by manpower, they could not come too close under sail. The ships were moving slowly as the oarsmen got their rhythm and they crept toward the quay. They could make out what must have been lanterns on top of posts which lined the edge of the quay. All the crew's attention was now on the task ahead, docking both ships. Jasper picked up rope, tied it to a belaying pin which was in a socket on the ship's rail and dropped the other end overboard.

The small sailing boat came alongside, on the starboard, right-hand side, tied up to the Pelican and El Conde leaned over and called out in English. A seaman spoke back and a two way conversation began. Jasper explained that this would be the pilot whose job it was to approach all incoming ships, guide them to a dock and charge them a landing fee.

Jack and Tom made the most of this distraction and went behind a set of steps on the port side, which led up onto the raised deck at the stern of the Pelican. They quickly took off their shoes, tied the laces together, undid their belts and looped the shoes through the back. Jasper and Kate stood with their backs to the boys hiding them from view, in case any of the crew turned and looked their way.

Ready for their escape, they gave Jasper and Kate a quick hug and thanked them in whispered voices, "We're very grateful, see you soon err… we hope." Tom's voice broke slightly. They shook hands with Jasper, kissed Kate briefly on the cheek and said their farewells.

"You've been good friends. Thank you so much. Goodbye… for now!"

At that, Jack climbed over the bulwark promptly followed by Tom. Standing on a protruding ledge just below the bulwark, they clung onto the rope and one behind the other, Tom going first, walked horizontally down the side of the ship as if they were abseiling. When they were a few feet above the water, they dropped in one after the other.

Having talked about it beforehand, they swam at right angles away from the ship, which was leaving them behind as it was steadily towed towards Port Royal. Once a hundred yards from the travelling direction of the ship, they angled their swimming back towards land aiming for a point a good distance from the quay that The Pelican and San Francisco were aiming for.

"How are you doing Tom?" Jack was tiring. They were both doing a steady breaststroke, quite slowly because of their clothes and shoes weighing them down.

"OK," Tom gasped. "But my shoes are filled with water and creating a bit of a drag. How about you?"

Jack panted, "OK, same with me, getting tired but I'll make it."

The dark area at the end of the lighted quay was getting closer. The wind was off the land and the boys could smell food cooking and hear voices. This seemed to spur them on. They quickened their strokes and within another ten minutes or so were just yards from their landing point. As they approached, they could see steps leading up from the water to the quay. Small boats crowded the area near the bottom of the steps and they had to push their way through them. Pausing and listening as they didn't want to be seen coming out of the water, they nodded to each other and climbed the steps. They crouched behind some huge barrels stacked on the edge of the dock emptied the water from their shoes and put them on.

"Right," said Jack, "let's make a dash for that alleyway over there. We'll try to get our bearings once we're off this quayside."

"OK, let's go!" Tom was off and running, Jack close behind.

They reached the alley and stopped. In between two sets of buildings it was actually a street, lit with what must have been some sort of oil lamps on the tops of poles about ten feet high. There were what looked to be houses on either side of the street and a tavern or some sort of pub a short distance from where they had stopped running. They could hear singing and loud voices coming from within. Two men, staggering, holding on to each other stumbled out of the tavern. Jack and Tom stepped into a doorway into the shadows with their backs leaning up against a door. Suddenly, the door they were leaning on was pulled open from the inside and the boys fell over backwards into the vestibule of the house or whatever it was, crashing onto a stone floor.

A huge voice bellowed, "Well me hearties! What can I do for 'ee hidin' in me doorway? I saw 'ee from my window at the front comin' up from the water and skulkin' around. Are 'ee up to no good?"

The boys were horrified. They stood, dripping water onto the floor. Their future flashed before their eyes. In front of them was a large man and he could not have been more typical of a story book pirate. He had a beard, a patch over one eye, a hook for one of his hands and a wooden peg leg, supported by a "T" shaped crutch, like Long John Silver in the book "Treasure Island". He was obviously English. They just stared, mouths open.

"Well! Speak up lads. What are 'ee doin'?"

It was Tom who spoke first. "Err… well, sir, we were captured by a pirate, Edward Boyle, and then after a sea battle, we were taken by some Spaniards and we've escaped by swimming ashore."

Jack pitched in, "Yes, sir, the Spaniards were going to sail us back to England and we really need to go to Pigeon Island so we can make our own way home."

"Well now, there's a interestin' story. Cap'n Edward Boyle? What 'appened to 'im then?"

The boys spoke as one. "He's dead!" Jack carried on. "The Spaniards set a trap and filled their ship with a company of soldiers who easily overcame Boyle and his pirates."

"Dead is 'ee now? I suppose I could take you both along to that pair o' ships I saw comin' in and ask for meself. What do yer think?"

"Please sir, no! The Spaniards will take us prisoner again. We have two friends on board who had been captured by the pirates, whose father, Sir James Bennett has a plantation here on Jamaica. They're being let go and we have arranged to meet them at their father's home."

"Sounds reasonable. Easily confirmed by takin' you to the plantation in the mornin'."

He went on, "Sir James Bennett? A fine man. I sailed with him in the British Navy for three years. I 'ad to retire with my injuries and I live 'ere now. Made some money from some sugar meself after I left the navy, that's 'ow I came to live in this fine 'ouse. Sir James settled 'ere when 'ee left the navy, a man of some wealth, 'ee is."

Being taken to Sir James' plantation next morning? The boy's hopes rose again.

"Come inside 'ee pair o' ragamuffins. Let's get 'ee dry and get some vittles into 'ee."

Jack and Tom followed behind and they went into a large room, the centrepiece of which was a huge fireplace with some meat on a spit over glowing coals.

"Get them wet things off and 'ang em on those lines on the sides of the fire, I'll find 'ee somethin' to put on."

The old seaman limped off. They did as they were told and waited. Clump, thump, footstep, clump, thump footstep, his crutch hit the stone floor, then his peg leg, then his good foot, as he came back. He was carrying two long shirts, "I reckon these 'ere will do 'ee till yer clothes are dry." Jack and Tom put them on and laughed. They were like old-fashioned nightshirts. "By the way, I'm Will Hardcastle, yer can call me Will."

The boys introduced themselves and thanked Will for letting them into his home. They were told to sit at the table and served with some pork, which the roasting meat turned out to be, a lump of hard bread and a small tankard of ale which the boys thought tasted disgusting. This was fresh pork though, rather than the salt meat they had been having onboard ship and was a pleasant change.

They told their story, leaving out the "Time Cave" as they had started calling the whole reason they were in their current situation. Will was impressed that they had survived.

Tom, curious said, "I hope you don't mind me asking Will, but what happened to your leg?"

He shifted in his armchair. "Well me lads, when I was on me old ship HMS Devonshire, we was in action against some pirates and a cannonball took it clean off below the knee."

Jack chimed in. "That's awful! It must have been a terrifying experience. But what happened to your hand? You've got a hook."

"Aye, right you are. Lost me 'and in a fight with some of the fiercest pirates this side of the Spanish Main. Repellin' boarders, one of them blaggards swung his cutlass and took it clean off at the wrist. 'ence the 'ook."

"Wow! You certainly went through some terrible times Will. But why the eye patch?"

"Ah yes. I was at the ship's helm one time. We was cuttin' along in a fair breeze, I was enjoyin' the day and I looked up at the sky and a seagull pooped in my eye."

Tom looked aghast. Jack's mouth was working but no words came out. Tom spoke up.

"You lost an eye from err… seagull poop?"

Will leaned forward, "Err… No. It was me first day with me 'ook."

He went into great guffaws of laughter. Pleased with himself. The boys stared at Will, puzzled, then it dawned on them he had poked out his own eye with the hook when he automatically reached to wipe his eye. They both started to laugh, realising that this was most likely his party-piece joke and was probably untrue. The sense of relief at being somewhere safe relaxed them and they found it hard to stop laughing.

The evening flew by as the old rogue regaled the boys with stories of his adventures with the British Navy. Pirates, battles with the Spanish fleet, his warship acting as escort to many flotillas of settlers to the British colonies along the eastern seaboard of what would become the United States of America. Jack and Tom were fascinated. Three-hundred-year-old history lessons from someone who had actually been there.

"Right, me lads let's get some sleep and we'll see if we can get you to Sir James' plantation tomorrow, eh?" Will hauled himself to his feet and motioned for the boys to follow him. He led them along a stone floored corridor and pushed open a heavy door. In the room there was a large bed, the mattress of which was so high off the floor there was a wooden platform which obviously acted as a step to help climb onto it.

"Climb aboard lads, I'll see yer in the mornin'. Sleep well."

"Thanks Will."

Both boys were ready for bed, the first real bed they'd had the chance to sleep in since leaving home. With what they had been through it all seemed a lifetime ago. They climbed up and onto the mattress, pulling back the covers. There was a musty smell, the bed felt a bit damp, which was probably because of the high humidity in the tropics. The boys didn't care and sleep came quickly.

Six

The next thing they knew was when Will shook them awake. "Come on me hearties, rise and shine." They could see daylight leaking in around the window shutters. "Yer clothes is dry, 'ere they be, go on and get dressed and I'll get 'ee some vittles." He clumped off leaving them to get up.

"I'm dying for a pee Tom, where do you think we go?" Jack looked around the room as if there might be an en-suite bathroom.

Tom got down on his hands and knees and looked under the bed and then stretched his arm, reaching for something. "Here, a chamber pot." He gave a little giggle. This was novel for both of them but they relieved themselves, got dressed and went back to the main room where Will was busy, slicing some meat off the pork joint from last evening. He dropped a piece each onto plates along with a slice of bread.

"Sit lads, get this down 'ee and I'll organise gettin' 'ee to Sir James's plantation." He spooned what the boys now recognised as mollasses onto his bread, put the meat on it, folded the bread in half and took a huge bite. The boys followed suit and although strange to have sweetness with savoury food it wasn't unpleasant. They'd had worse over the past week or so.

Will mopped his plate with a remaining piece of bread, wiped his mouth with the back of his hand, burped and said, "I'll go out and make some arrangements for 'ee. I'll be back in a short while."

"Oh, what is it you have to do?" Jack asked.

Will paused, as if he didn't expect the question, his answer was a little hesitant. "Err… I'm going to seek out an old shipmate who will take 'ee to Sir James." He stood, balanced himself with his crutch and limped to the front door. "Don't step outside, 'ee don't want to be seen."

He went out the door and closed it behind him. The boys looked at each other. Tom spoke up first. "Do you think Will was a bit strange there. Can we trust him?"

Jack agreed. "Let's look outside. I'll look along the quay and you look up the street to see if he's gone in another direction."

They leapt up from the table and moved quickly to the door. Outside Tom turned left and kept close into the buildings. Jack crossed the narrow street and stopped at the corner so he could look along the quay towards the San Francisco and The Pelican. He lay prostrate on the stone cobbles and just put his right eye around the corner. Limping and shuffling along the cobbled quayside ahead was Will Hardcastle. He was going as quickly as his disability would allow him. He was glancing back over his shoulder.

"Tom!" Jack hissed. "Get over here!" Tom was only a short distance up the street and he quickly dashed over to Jack. "Here, lie down and you'll see Will. He looks very suspicious."

Tom lay where Jack had been and looked along the quay. "He's boarding the Spanish ship. I think he's giving us up!"

Jack stepped out and looked towards the two ships tied up to the dock. "Yes! I think you're right!" They maintained their vigil for the next few minutes until they spotted the unmistakable figure of El Conde running down the gangplank followed by a group of Spanish soldiers.

"Let's go Tom!" The boys dashed up the street. "Wait a second I'll lock the door, it might slow them down."

Jack took the huge key from the inside the huge front door, pulled it shut, turned the key, put it in his pocket and they set off like olympic sprinters. Reaching the end of the street they hid briefly to look back to see the soldiers rounding the corner. They set off along another street having turned left, running as if their lives depended on it, which of course it did.

The soldiers led by El Conde went slowly to Will Hardcastle's front door. El Conde knocked on the door and waited. He tapped again. As he waited, Will came limping round the corner and up to the door.

"He whispered, leave it to me sir." In a louder voice he said, "Come on lads. It's me, Will." Nothing. He banged the door very hard. "Open up boys. It's alright, it's me, Will."

"It seems like your 'lads' have either decided to lock themselves in, or run away." El Conde looked with distaste at Will. He turned to the soldiers behind him and issued an order in rapid Spanish. Two soldiers stepped forward and using the butts of their muskets, smashed the window to the side of the door.

"What are you doin'? Yer smashin' my 'ouse up!" Will was incensed, he pushed forward but was kept back by a couple of burly soldiers. He kept shouting, his distress obvious. People started coming out of their doors to see what the disturbance was.

Two soldiers climbed in through the the broken window and disappeared into the house. After a few minutes they came back shaking their heads. They climbed back out and reported to El Conde.

The Spaniard turned to Will Hardcastle and said, "Well, we do know where they are going. We will find them."

Will's betrayal of the boys was all about money. He had lulled them into a false sense of security so he could hand them over to the Spaniards for reward.

"What about me money? You wouldn't 'ave known where they were or where they were goin' if I hadn't told 'ee!"

"Well, Senor Hardcastle, we obviously do not have the boys and your plan did not work in our favour. So we still have much work to do to find them, so goodbye. We owe you nothing!"

Will, muttering under his breath made his way to his broken window, where with some difficulty he managed to climb in by sitting on the sill and edging his body inside. El Conde headed back towards his ship at a brisk pace followed by his men.

Jack and Tom headed west. The map Jasper had drawn for them was smudged and the ink had run so some of it was illegible but the basis of it and the landscape as described by Jasper was stuck in Jack's head. He had memorised the detail in case this happened when they swam ashore. They were out of the town now, in open country, making their way to Spy Glass Hill, the highest point in this part of the island, which was their main reference point, leaving the town. Once over it they would be able to see the eastern boundary of Old Sussex Hall, the Bennett's sugar plantation.

The countryside was lush and green with palm trees dotted here and there. They passed a big plantation house on the south side of the road. It looked very colonial, painted white and they could see one end of what looked like a verandah along the front edge. Large flowering shrubs grew alongside the house and a huge green lawn spread out to the front. Black workers tended the gardens, hoeing, digging and cutting.

It dawned on the boys, "Those people are slaves Tom!" Jack's voice was incredulous.

"You took the words out of my mouth. Of course, slavery hadn't been abolished in 1720."

Tom and Jack remembered their history lessons about the major European seafaring nations, Spain, Portugal, France and Britain, in collusion with some West African Kings, kidnapping African natives and shipping them to the Americas packed tightly into the holds of sailing ships, many of them dying horrible deaths because of the appalling conditions. Then in many cases, living in terrible and cruel conditions as slaves on plantations.

"It's awful, Jack. But at least we know slavery ended. There's nothing to be done for over a hundred years, more's the pity."

The sea was to their left. The ground rose gently to their right and in front. About a mile ahead, it got steeper as Spy Glass Hill got closer. It was hot and humid and the sun burned through their shirts, it was hard going.

Tom broke the silence, "Why do you think it's so important for El Conde to catch us, Jack?"

"I don't know. I've been thinking about that. Maybe it's a pride thing. Perhaps he feels we've cheated him out of getting some praise and recognition for bringing us home after being kidnapped by pirates?"

Jack was pensive for a moment. "I think you're right. As El Conde said the other day, he wants to impress his bosses and his King. His pride is injured because we've escaped, so he's determined to catch us. Let's not give him a chance to prove us right or wrong on what his reasons are. C'mon let's keep going."

After about twenty minutes of striding out, they started to climb the lower slopes of Spy Glass Hill. They were tiring, the baking sun was hammering down. Thirsty and becoming dehydrated, the heat and energy they were expending was taking it out of them. They reached a cluster of boulders, set in a circle, almost as if they had been arranged there by a giant hand.

"Let's have a quick break eh Tom?"

"I didn't want to say it first but yes. Just a couple of minutes."

The boys sank to the ground, sitting on rough grass, their backs against a boulder. As they began to relax, slightly out of breath from their steady climb, it was silent apart from a breeze rustling vegetation and birds calling. Jack suddenly stood back up.

"Can you hear water running Tom?" Tom climbed to his feet and looked in the same direction as Jack.

"Yes, from over there!" He pointed towards a line of trees over to their right. "It must be a stream! Come on, let's have a look."

They started to run, their thirst now a driving force. Breaking through the trees, before them was the most wonderful sight. At the bottom of a deep sloping riverbank was a crystal clear, rocky stream gushing and gurgling its way downhill. The boys almost fell down the bank and jumped in up to their ankles, knelt down on the pebbles and stones and drank like animals, faces in the water. Cold and delicious, they sated their thirst. They then turned on their backs and let the water run over them, cooling themselves off. It was heaven.

After a few moments they sat up, smiling and feeling much better. They were on their way to freedom. They were hopeful that Sir James would get them back to Pigeon Island and they could reverse their situation and return to the twenty-first century and home.

They heard a voice, in the distance but definitely a human voice. They looked at one another, then edged their way up the riverbank to the trees, crawling like commandoes. Lying face down in the shade of the trees they looked across the open ground towards the group of boulders where they had been sitting earlier. It was El Conde and ten of his soldiers. One of the soldiers was holding a scrap of paper and showing it to El Conde.

"It's El Conde and his men!"

Jack could not believe their bad luck, he felt in his pocket but the map Jasper had given them was gone. He had dropped it. Now the Spaniards knew where they were heading although he was sure that Will must have given the game away.

"How does he dare do this? This is a British Colony and the Spaniards are running around as if they own it. Surely they can't do that?"

"No good worrying about that, Jack. They want us and at this point I don't think I want to have an argument about the rights and wrongs of chasing British subjects. Let's go!"

"Yes! Let's stay under cover of these trees as far as we can and carry on up the stream bed."

They set off, trying to keep the noise levels down as the waded through the water, luckily only up to their knees in places. Standing on loose stones and slippery rocks made their ascent difficult but fear spurred them on. They did not want to be caught.

Stopping occasionally, they went up to the treeline and looked at the Spaniards who were keeping a parallel course and heading in the same general direction as them.

"I hope they don't decide to come over here, Jack. I'm surprised they haven't." Tom kept his voice low.

"It seems to me that knowing where we're going, they think they'll catch up with us sooner rather than later. I'm pretty sure they wouldn't try to take us from Sir James' home if we get there first."

Tom responded, "I wouldn't bet on it. Those guys are heavily armed with muskets and swords. Sir James only has his plantation workers, I would guess. Anyway, we're going to have to break cover at some stage. Let's keep going."

The stream bed was getting steeper. Cut into the hillside, the tumbling water was making it difficult walking in parts where the current was strong over the loose rocks and stones.

Occasionally the boys slipped and fell and had to stifle a yelp of pain as they bashed their knees or shins. They were making slow progress and it was evident that if the Spaniards were getting ahead of them, at this rate they would be waiting at the gates of the plantation for them. They just had to arrive first.

Jack had an idea. "Tom, let's get out of the stream and get up on the bank to our right here. The trees line the edge, all along the top of the riverbank. With the trees on the lefthand side as well, they shouldn't be able to see us. It's a risk but we need to move faster."

Tom thought a moment, looking right and then left at the trees. "Yeah, OK. Let's give it a try."

The boys scrambled up the bank and got themselves on the outside of the line of trees. Moving slowly, they glanced to their left and although there was the odd gap where they could be seen through both sets of trees, they couldn't see the Spaniards. They began to run. The ground was getting steeper and soon they were panting for breath in the hot humid atmosphere. After a few hundred yards they stopped and after a brief conversation, Jack slid down the bank to the stream and then climbed up the other side. Hidden behind a tree trunk he looked down the hill. Further down the slope, El Conde and his men had stopped and were sitting and two of them were carrying what looked like goatskin water carriers towards the stream. The boys had seen and used goatskins onboard ship so Jack knew immediately that they were coming to collect water. He scrambled back down into the stream and climbed up the other side, through the trees and when Tom saw Jack he leapt to his feet, his face anxious.

Out of breath Jack told Tom what he'd seen.

"We've got to get a move on, come on!"

Tom was up and didn't need to be told again. They were off like greyhounds, as fast as the slope would allow them. It was hard work but they were covering ground and putting distance between themselves and the Spaniards. Suddenly and without warning, two Spanish soldiers stepped out of the trees in front of them. They had been outsmarted. Jack hadn't even thought to count the resting group sitting with El Conde. Two of them had got up the hill on the other side of the stream ahead of them, crossed over and waited for them. They had known all along what the boys were doing and where they were. The two soldiers were grinning from ear to ear.

"Buenas Dias, muchachos."

Jack and Tom were dumbfounded. Their hopes of getting home had disappeared in a split second. The soldiers grabbed them by the backs of their tee shirts and started towards the top of the river bank between the trees. One of them raised his musket in the air and fired a shot. The crack resounded like thunder and birds rose in the air from the trees, squawking in alarm. The boys both jumped in shock. This was a signal to their comrades, no doubt.

Jack said, "Tom, remember what I did when we managed to trip that Spaniard overboard during the sea battle? When I say, now, do it. OK?"

Tom remembered immediately. How could he forget, they had probably drowned someone. He nodded almost imperceptibly just as one of the soldiers said in a harsh voice, "Silenzio!"

The boys understood what that meant, fortunately these Spaniards didn't understand English.

They were being pushed to the edge of the steep bank above the stream and just at the beginning of the slope, Jack cried out, "Now!" and both boys dropped simultaneously to their hands and knees. The soldiers barged into the boys' bodies and tumbled over them yelling in shock and anger. Their ribs were whacked by the Spaniards shins as they went over but what they saw next was worth the pain. Their capturers somersaulted down the slope, rolling over several times before crashing into the stream. It had all happened in seconds. They had both dropped their muskets as they fell, throwing out their arms in a reaction to falling. The one closest to Tom hadn't been fired so he picked it up. Jack picked up the other which might serve as a club.

"Let's go!" was the victory cry.

Pleased with themselves, hope returned. Off they went again, up the hill, running, lungs bursting. Hearing shouts, they looked back over their shoulders and saw El Conde and his men at the point where the soldiers had fallen.

Jack and Tom kept running. The top of Spy Glass Hill seemed to be getting closer. Looking back again they saw a group of four soldiers coming after them, labouring up the hill, at least two hundred yards behind. El Conde and the rest of his men seemed to have disappeared.

Reaching a huge rocky outcrop, covering an area of about four hundred yards across and a hundred yards running up the slope, with shale, rubble and boulders strewn around, Jack had an idea.

"Come on Tom, let's get to the top of these rocks as quickly as we can. I've got a plan to slow them down."

Scrambling over boulders and large rocks it was hard going and slower than climbing the grassy hill but after about five minutes, they made it to the top edge of the outcrop.

"Right, stop here and see if we can't send a few boulders onto them."

"Great idea Jack! What about this one?"

They stopped by a boulder about a metre across and got down on their knees, shoulders to the rather large rock and heaved. It was so heavy but it moved slightly, sliding on the loose shale underneath it. Straining, Tom thought his eyes were going to pop out. Jack felt as if his shoulder pushing against the rock was going to break. Suddenly, they both pitched forward onto their faces as the boulder took off, tumbling, gaining speed and momentum, hitting other smaller rocks and sending them crashing down the hill. The hapless Spaniards coming up the hill looked up and saw what was happening. Their faces reflected the horror of the situation. The huge boulder was almost upon them as they split up and started running back down the hill at an angle from what was becoming a stony avalanche. A chain rection had begun. One rock hit another, then dislodged others and it was quickly raining stone. Some of the smaller rocks caught the escaping soldiers' legs and feet and sent them tumbling. Hurt but in great fear for their lives they kept getting up and running down the hill.

Elated, Jack and Tom turned and ran as hard as they could up the hill, not wasting anytime to look back, they felt they had made up some distance by slowing up their pursuers. Eventually reaching the top of the hill, they paused, looking down at the vista in front of them. About a mile ahead was a stone wall surrounding a vast area of cultivation. Fields of tall bamboo-like plants, what the boys guessed must be sugar-cane, seemed to go on forever. There was a gateway in the wall, with a palm tree lined drive running in a straight line to a very large colonial style house, which looked to Tom like some of the large stately homes he had visited with his parents back in England. He felt a wave of sadness sweep over him at the thought.

He spoke in an emotional voice, "That house looks just like…"

Jack interrupted, "I know, I know, don't say any more." He looked rather downcast but his expression changed rapidly, as he said suddenly, "Look, Tom! El Conde has come around the side of the hill with the rest of his men!"

There to their left and too close for comfort were the Spanish soldiers, making good progress to cut them off. They heard El Conde give an order. At that, two of the soldiers dropped to one knee and fired their muskets in the boy's general direction. They heard the musket balls whizz by some distance away. These were obviously warning shots to make them stop and give up. They both knew that the accuracy of muskets was rather erratic so weren't too worried about being shot at that distance.

Tom still carrying the musket he had picked up when they tripped their erstwhile capturers, brought it to his shoulder and aimed at the Spaniards. On seeing this, the Spaniards dropped to the ground, taking cover.

"Don't shoot, Tom," hissed Jack. "Save your shot in case we really need it!"

Muskets could only be fired once and then had to be reloaded with powder and shot before being any use again.

"It's OK Jack, I wasn't going to. I just wanted to scare them."

"Okay! Let's see if we can outrun them down this way." Jack started off to their right, down what was the western slope of Spy Glass Hill.

Tom caught up as they went quickly; galloping, jumping and tumbling over, getting up again and running for all they were worth. Glancing back at the Spaniards below them, they could see their pursuers were keeping a line along the hillside to intersect with them. They ran harder. Ahead of them they could see a rocky promontory. This feature projected out for about three hundred yards, was a hundred yards wide and on the side the soldiers were approaching, it was a sheer wall of stone, a cliff face probably fifty feet in height. The Spaniards would have to climb it, then retrace their steps and come up the hill to get at the same level as the boys or go down the slope parallel with the rock wall to get around it to come up the other side.

"We can fool them here Tom! Let's keep going and let them think we are carrying on to the north, they will probably think they will meet us somewhere down the hill. We'll disappear out of site from them when we go to the right of the outcrop because they won't be able to see us from below the cliff. When they go around the end of the outcrop, we can change direction, retrace our steps and go straight down the hill to the plantation!"

"Good idea, Jack Let's do it!"

As Jack and Tom started to their right, The Spaniards looked up at the boys and chose the route taking them down the hill to attempt to cut the boys off, knowing that at some point they were going to have to head down towards the plantation. The boys kept going, running out of sight from the Spaniards who were somewhere below, on the right hand side of the rocky promontory.

After a few minutes, the boys stopped, panting and sweating in the ferocious sun. Waiting a while longer, they turned back and reached a point where they could look down along the left hand edge of the cliff face to where it ended. The Spaniards weren't in sight. They had traversed the bottom end of the promontory to get around the other side, hoping to cut off Tom and Jack. Now, turning back they carried on until they had left the rocky area behind them, the boys then started down the hill towards the plantation gates. Running hard, they covered the ground quickly. Lungs bursting, legs tiring, they knew they couldn't stop.

Glancing over his shoulder towards the rocks, Tom yelled, "They're coming down the hill, Jack! They've seen us!"

"Come on Tom, we can make it, keep going!"

El Conde had obviously deduced that the boys had tricked them and he and his men had come back from the blind side of the promontory to spot them tearing down the hill towards the plantation gateway. The Spaniards were running but hampered by their knee-high boots and their armoured breastplates weighing them down. They were a good distance behind Jack and Tom.

The hillside stared to level off, the boys were approaching the massive gates, the entrance to the plantation. They slowed, their legs on fire with muscle fatigue and crossed a road which was no more than dried earth, and trotted through the gates and onto the driveway.

"We still have a mile or so to get to the house, we can't stop or slow down too much or those guys will catch up to us!" Jack was stating the obvious.

They had slowed though, their aching legs and burning lungs wouldn't allow them to maintain any faster speed. They were jogging, the drive seemed like a marathon, the huge house at the end of the drive didn't seem to be getting any closer. Hearing shouts behind them, they turned and looked back. The Spanish soldiers were onto the drive and getting closer. Sheer willpower kept them going, they were physically exhausted but getting home was the driving force. They were, they felt, only a few hundred yards from achieving part of that goal.

They were approaching the house now with their pursuers not far behind them. They couldn't see anyone, not a soul anywhere in front of them. As they jogged into the large open area which surrounded the house at the end of the drive, a sudden tumult erupted behind them. Turning, they saw dozens of plantation workers coming from the cane on either side of the drive, armed with pitchforks, machetes, some with muskets, they completely surrounded the Spaniards in moments. A tall man closely followed by Jasper made his way into the middle of the plantation workers where the Spaniards stood, motionless, looking very unhappy. This was obviously Sir James Bennett with his son Jasper. The boys walked back to see what was going on.

"Who is in charge here?" Sir James voice was authoritative.

"It is I, El Conde Fernan Gonzalez. At your service, Sir." He bowed with a flourish, taking off his hat.

"You are Spanish sir. I demand to know what you are doing, in a British colony, pursuing British subjects?"

"Well, Sir James, we rescued these boys and of course your own children from vicious pirates. As you know, we released your children into the custody of your representative yesterday, and they are now home safe with you. The boys, Jack and Tom, we wish to take home to Cornwall in England, from whence they came. This was a generous gesture on my part to prove that we Spanish are glad to be at peace once more with England. These boys have made fools of me by running away. I have informed the King of Spain that I am taking them to England and so it shall be. I will not have such ungracious and ungrateful behaviour towards me. I would like you to hand them over to me, now, if you please."

"I extend my gratitude to you for rescuing my children, but I will not hand over these boys to you under any circumstances, you are an arrogant peacock sir, looking to somehow enhance your reputation with this ridiculous plan. Have you nothing better to do? I will have none of it. Now turn around and leave my property and return to your ship. I will be talking with the Governor about this and ask him to have a word with His Excellency the Spanish Ambassador."

El Conde, his pride hurt, put his nose in the air, barked an order, turned on his heel and set off down the drive with his men following. Sir James told his workers to disperse and go back to their duties.

Jasper was just in the process of introducing Jack and Tom to his father, when Tom suddenly dropped to one knee, aimed and fired his musket. Everyone spun around to see a Spanish soldier falling to the ground. As he fell, the soldier's musket which had obviously been in the firing position dropped from his hands as he clutched at his upper left arm, blood pouring from a wound. There was shocked silence until Sir James' workers reappeared as if by magic to surround the remaining soldiers.

"Tell your men to drop their weapons El Conde," yelled Sir James.

A quick terse order from El Conde and the soldiers dropped their muskets. Sir James strode over to El Conde. He was a tall imposing figure, probably in his late forties.

He stood close to El Conde and in barely disguised anger said, "That sir, was an act of war. Your man was attempting to kill one of us, probably me and if it hadn't been for the prompt action of this boy, one of us would likely be dead. What have you got to say for yourself?"

"Sir James, I swear to you on all that is holy that I did not order this act. He is a hot-headed young man who acted without thought or instruction. He will be taken back, court martialed and probably hanged. We are not here to jeopardise the peace between our two countries, sir. I promise you."

"Well, you could have fooled me. Once I have spoken to the Governor and he relays what I tell him to your superiors, I suspect any good deeds you have done of late will be cancelled out by your foolish behaviour here today. Get out of my sight!"

The wounded man was being attended to by one of his comrades, tying a neckerchief around his arm; and as that was completed, El Conde, looking extremely angry, ordered his men to follow him. They trudged off down the drive, looking rather chastened.

Tom looked ill. The blood had drained from his face. "I've just shot someone! I've just shot someone!" He was slightly unsteady on his feet.

Sir James put his arm around Tom's shoulders and supported him. It looked like he might be in mild shock.

"You did well there Tom. If you hadn't reacted so quickly, one of us could be dead by now. I'm very grateful to you. Come on lad, you did the right thing, just as well you had that musket, err, where did you come upon it? It's Spanish by the look of it."

"Two Spanish soldiers caught us and we managed to escape from them taking their muskets," chirped Jack.

Sir James was impressed, "Excellent work, gentlemen."

Jack continued, "Tom you're a hero, that was brilliant! I can't wait to tell our friends…" His voice trailed off, realising what he had just said. Tom gave him a rather scathing look. Who would believe them?

"Right, gentlemen, come, let's go into the house and we can eat and drink to celebrate your victory over the Spaniards." Sir James led them to the front doors of the very grand house. There were six stone steps which went from the gravelled turning circle up to the entrance. They walked through a vestibule and into a large room with a very high ceiling. It was a magnificent house, truly a stately home.

As they arrived, Kate entered from a hallway and her smile lit up the room as she saw Jack and Tom.

"You are safe. I'm delighted to see you both, you must tell us your adventures after leaving the ship. What was the gunfire I heard a little while ago, was it…?"

"One thing at a time Kate," Sir James interrupted. "Please ask Gabriel to draw a bath for these young gentlemen, then perhaps a shirt and a pair of britches each from Jasper's wardrobe, which will be a little on the large side but will do for now. They can have their rather err… ahem… well, their current wardrobe laundered." Kate curtsied to her father and went off back down the hallway.

"There's no need to go to any trouble for us, Sir James," Jack was slightly embarrassed.

"Nonsense! I won't hear of it. Come, let's go on to the kitchen where you can have some liquid refreshment and a bite to eat. You can join us all for dinner tonight." Sir James was used to people doing his bidding.

They trooped behind him, along the hall to a huge kitchen which was about fifty feet square. Large cast iron cooking ranges lined one wall, wooden cabinets ran up each of the adjacent walls and three doors about two yards apart took up some of the remaining wall. One of these doors was open and it was evident from the goods inside that this was a pantry. The boys assumed that the other doors opened to something similar. In the middle of the floor was a very large table on which food was being prepared by two women. This was a kitchen on an industrial scale, big enough to create a feast for many guests. There were six staff at work, peeling some strange-looking vegetables and some of which were recognisable to Jack and Tom. They all stopped and the women, four of them curtsied and the men bowed to Sir James.

"Carry on, please. Martha could you give these boys a drink and a slice of beef and bread? I'll leave them in your hands. Jasper, please take them to their rooms after they've eaten, their baths should be ready. I'll see you all at dinner. I'm off to Kingston for a plantation owners meeting this afternoon. Good day to you, young gentlemen and thank you once again

Tom for your timely intervention." At that Sir James turned and left the kitchen.

Jasper had a word with Martha that the boys couldn't hear and then asked that they follow him, which they did. Turning out of the kitchen they went through a large reception room. The room was furnished with what they would describe as antiques in the twenty-first century but were probably modern in this century. There were several painted portraits hung on each wall. They were all pictures of very grand-looking gentlemen, some in military uniform and some in clothes which were obviously fashionable at the time the portraits were painted. Stepping through some french windows they found themselves on a paved terrace. Jasper invited the boys to sit at an oblong wooden table with six matching chairs. The table was shaded by a canvas awning supported by a wooden framework of upright and horizontal posts. A warm breeze made the awning flap.

"Sounds like the sails of The Pelican, Tom."

"I was just thinking the same."

Jasper smiled, almost to himself as he took a seat beside the boys. At that Martha came out, carrying a large tray with a large jug of water, glasses and plates of bread and slices of beef.

She set the tray down on the table, grinning from ear to ear, said in a voice that was full of humour and wonderful Jamaican accent, "Right now gentlemen, enjoy dis and let me know if der's anyt'ing else you'll be needin'?"

Jasper said, "Thank you Martha, I'm sure this will be fine, I don't think we'll need anything else." Both boys thanked her too and Martha nodded, smiled at the boys and returned back indoors.

Jasper handed out the plates of food, poured water into glasses which the boys gratefully guzzled down and went back for more. It had been a long hard morning. They tucked in to the beef and bread, they were hungry as usual.

Between mouthfuls, Jack spoke up. "Jasper, we can't thank you and your father enough for your hospitality and kindness. Err… is your mother here?"

"Our mother died shortly after Kate was born. Our father sent us to school in England when we were old enough. We come back here once a year during our school recess."

Jack was embarrassed, "I'm so sorry Jasper, I didn't know."

Jasper smiled reassuringly, "It's err… okay," Jasper smiled at his own use of the boy's peculiar expression. "How could you have known?"

They all continued with their lunch without further conversation until Tom asked, "Jasper, how can your father help us get back to Pigeon Island? Does he have a boat or ship that could take us?"

Jasper swallowed his mouthful of food, took a drink of water, then replied. "My father has several large ships he uses to transport sugar to England. He also has a Bermuda rigged sloop he could use to take you. It depends on what routes he has planned, he has recently started trading with the British colonies in America."

"Bermuda rigged sloop, what's that?" Tom was curious.

"It's a boat about fifty feet long with two triangular sails, fast and very seaworthy. Father uses it for sailing between the islands. I'm sure by the time we have supper tonight, he will present you with a plan. I've told him about your 'magic' appearance through the cave at Pigeon Island. He's sceptical of course, but insists he wants to help you get home."

As they chatted, having finished their snack, Gabriel appeared at the table. "Excuse me young sirs, but the baths are ready for Mr Jack and Mr Tom. If you are ready, please follow me."

Jasper spoke up, "Thank you Gabriel, I'm sure Jack and Tom will be delighted to follow you. There's been something of a err… strange smell in the house since they arrived." A mischievous smile appeared and he gave a little giggle, teasing Tom and Jack.

This was the first time the boys had heard Jasper really laugh. He was obviously relaxed being at home, they wished they could say the same. However, they had to admit that apart from the swim to the dock from The Pelican, their bodies had not been immersed in water for over a week. They must smell badly and would relish a warm bath. They found it hard to believe they had a butler looking after them!

Gabriel had the full dress and livery of a butler of the time period. Long coat with gold braid and brass buttons, knee britches, long socks and buckled shoes, all topped of with a white wig that ended in a sort of pony tail. They followed him upstairs where he showed each of them into a bedroom. On each of their respective beds, a shirt and breeches belonging to Jasper were laid out. In each room was a huge metal bathtub full of steaming water awaiting them.

Alone in their rooms, they tossed their clothes onto the floor then climbed into the wonderful warm water where using soap for the first time in over a week they scrubbed off their grubby bodies.

Having got himself clean with a huge bar of soap, Tom was relaxing in the bathtub in his room, he was surprised when a knock came on the door.

"Errr… yes?" Tom suddenly felt vulnerable in his present state.

"It's Mary sir, I've come to collect your clothes for the laundry. May I come in?"

A girl in the room when he was having a bath? Not likely, "Hold on! I'll let you in."

Tom stood up, grabbed the linen towel hanging on a hook on the wall next to the bath, dried himself as quickly as he could and dived into Jasper's clothes, which were a bit too big but would serve their purpose while their own clothes were being washed. Opening the door, he saw Mary waiting patiently. She didn't look any older than Tom and Jack.

"Please, help yourself," Tom stood to one side to let Mary pass. "I'll get Jack's clothes for you."

Tom went next door, gave a sharp knock and told Jack he wanted to come in to get his dirty clothes.

"No you'll have to wait until I've finished," was his reply.

"Okay, I'll let Mary come and do it then."

"What! A girl? What are you talking about?"

"Mary appears to be a maid who is doing our laundry. Either I collect your clothes or she does." Tom was enjoying this.

"Okay, you do it."

Tom entered the room, grinning from ear to ear. Mary stood at the doorway, her back to the room, looking at the corridor wall. Collecting the clothes which were strewn on the floor just as his had been, he handed them to Mary, who went off along the corridor.

"Come on Jack, I'll see you downstairs."

Seven

Jack, wearing Jasper's clothes, walked into the reception room that led onto the terrace where they'd had lunch. Jasper and Tom were sitting in leather wing-back chairs facing each other, laughing at the story of Mary and their laundry.

"We're not used to servants, Jasper." Jack wasn't sure how to express his discomfort with slavery.

"Well, after living like animals on that pirate ship, I'm glad we've got them," Jasper responded.

Both Jack and Tom looked at each other, neither of them spoke though. They both knew what the other was thinking.

"Would you boys like to come to the beach and have a swim?" Jasper's voice was enthusiastic. "We can spend a few hours down there, do some fishing as well and come back for supper."

Jack and Tom didn't hesitate. Swimming and fishing were two of their favourite pastimes.

"Excellent idea Jasper, but we haven't any swimming shorts," chipped in Tom.

"Swimming shorts? I assume these are something you wear to swim in... err... where you live? Well I'm sure we can find you something."

"Okay! I've got an idea, we could take our underwear from the laundry. They are boxer shorts. Can we get them Jasper?"

"Boxer shorts?" Jasper looked perplexed but he was getting used to hearing the strange language the boys used on occasion. "Yes of course, even if they are wet it doesn't matter as you will be getting them wet anyway."

Jasper led the way through the house to an outbuilding at the back where several women were in various stages of the laundry process. One of them had a long pole, at the bottom of which was a copper bowl about a foot across with holes all over it, which she was holding in both hands and beating some clothes in steaming hot water inside a half barrel – a washtub. An eighteenth-century washing machine thought Jack. Nearby another woman was rinsing the washed laundry in clean water and next to her was a contraption similar to that the boys had seen in a visit to a museum, called a mangle or wringer. This consisted of two large rollers set in an iron frame which were turned by a handle on the outside. Wet washing was fed into the rollers, the handle turned and the water was squeezed out, making it easier to dry.

Looking in a basket near the washtub Tom picked out their boxer shorts. "Here we are, got'em, let's go chaps!"

Jasper picked up three towels which were in a pile of dry, clean laundry and then led the way to another outbuilding. This was storeroom of sorts and was stacked with a variety of objects. Jasper pointed to some long bamboo poles and on a shelf, some fishing line and a box of fishing hooks, lead weights and other fishing tackle.

"Choose three poles, boys, I'll bring the other equipment." Jasper picked up the box while Jack, not knowing whether there was any difference between the poles grabbed three of them and followed Jasper.

They took a well worn pathway between coconut palms that began to rise up a small incline. Rough grass covered the ground on either side of the track, vultures soared on the breeze, small birds flitted from tree to tree and the sun shone relentlessly. On reaching the top of the rising ground the land dropped away sweeping down to a white sand beach. The sea was turquoise close in to the beach and azure further out. Had it not been for the precarious situation of whether or not the boys would get home, this would have been idyllic. A great place to be on holiday. Still, they hoped to hear Sir James' plan this evening at supper. They would make the most of this time to have some fun, something they had not experienced of late.

They all started to trot down the hill, laughing and delighted to be free. Stopping at the waters edge, Jack and Tom changed into their underpants, while Jasper down to his.

The boys burst out into raucous laughter, pointing at Jasper who was wearing 'long johns,' underwear that went out of fashion probably a hundred years before the boys had been born! Jasper shook his head. He didn't even bother to say anything.

"Last one in stinks!" yelled Tom as he raced into the water, diving headfirst into a wave. Jack was close behind and Jasper, rather more of a gentleman walked in slowly. They were soon floating on their backs and enjoying the warm temperature of the Caribbean Sea. The water was only waist deep and they walked and swam out towards a coral reef that was a short distance offshore.

Swimming underwater, eyes open, Jack and Tom were in awe of the myriads of coloured fish darting around the coral. "I wish we had our goggles Tom," said Jack as he came up for air.

"I was just thinking that," replied Tom. "It's still fantastic though!"

After swimming and playing for a half hour or so, the three boys made their way back to the beach, where they sat for a while letting the sun dry them off. Sensibly they put on their shirts, the sun was fierce and none of them wanted to get sunburned. Jasper set up the fishing poles and from the box he'd brought with them, he picked out some small pieces of fish flesh which he attached to the hooks. These were truly primitive fishing rods with no reels, they were meant to be dangled in the water with about five yards of line and hope for the best. They had bottle corks as floats to keep the hook from sinking completely to the bottom. Following Jasper to an outcrop of rocks, they found a spot each and dropped the baited hooks and floats in the water.

The afternoon wore on, none of them had caught anything till Jasper cried, "Yes, I've got something!"

In just a few minutes, he had hauled in the fish, a decent size catch that Jasper said was a Parrot fish.

Shortly afterwards Jack and Tom were delighted to catch a fish each, Tom especially, as this was a Kingfish, large enough for a decent size meal. Jack's was another Parrot fish about the same size as Jasper's. Wrapping their catch in a water-soaked towel, Jasper put them in the box and suggested they go back to the house. After getting dressed, they set off back, very pleased with themselves.

On their return, they put away the fishing poles and went into the house where Jasper dropped off their catch in the kitchen.

"Come with me Jack, Tom, we must get the sand off our feet."

They had walked back barefoot and the sand was clinging to them almost up to their knees. Jasper strolled across the garden to a small stream on the other side. He stepped into the gurgling water and beamed with pleasure. Jack and Tom followed and the water was cool and felt wonderful on their feet and ankles. They could see why Jasper was smiling. They washed the sand from their legs and feet and walked back onto the lawn. The grass felt good under their toes.

"Let us see if we can get a drink from Gabriel. Sit down out here shall we?"

The boys took a seat where they'd had their lunch. Jasper strode indoors and rang a bell near the door. Within moments Gabriel appeared and Jasper said something to Gabriel, who nodded his head and retreated back inside the house. Jasper rejoined the pair and sat with them.

Tom said, "Today has seemed like a week. We've done so much. Run away from an old rogue sailor, been chased by Spaniards because their leader wanted some kind of praise or reward for returning us to England." He paused and took a breath, "Tripped two soldiers into a stream, stole their muskets, caused an avalanche and I shot and wounded one of the Spaniards. Had some lunch, had a bath, went for a swim caught some fish and are now waiting for a drink before supper! It's bizarre. You couldn't make it up!"

Jack shook his head in disbelief. "To complete our bizarre tale, add to that, being carried by an unstoppable current through a cave which turned out to be a tunnel, then sailing the Spanish Main after being kidnapped by pirates, fighting in a sea battle, then were kidnapped by the Spanish."

"Our parents will be frantic with worry. The police and air sea rescue would have been looking for us but I suppose they will have stopped after all this time. We have to get home."

"I truly don't understand the part about the cave; but much of the rest I have been through with you. My father will help you, I will come with you and make sure you get back through the cave." Jasper looked and sounded earnest. The boys had grown close, three friends who had overcome adversity together.

Gabriel carried in a tray with a jug of cloudy liquid and three glasses on it which he set down. Giving the boys a glass each he asked Jasper if there was anything else.

"No, thank you Gabriel, that will be all," came the reply.

Jasper filled their glasses with the cloudy liquid which had slices of lime in it. "This is lime juice and water mixed with a little sugar," said Jasper. "Give it a try."

It was delicious and cool, slightly sharp in taste but very refreshing. They quaffed it down and Jasper gave them each a refill.

They heard footsteps coming through the house. It was Sir James. Jasper stood up, Jack and Tom not sure what to do, got to their feet hesitantly.

"Ah here you are. Sit, gentlemen, please sit. Have you had a good afternoon? Young Jack and Tom, I trust you have been well looked after?"

Jack answered, "Yes sir, on behalf of both of us, thank you. We have had a wonderful afternoon. We've really enjoyed it."

"Good, good. You must come inside now, gentlemen. The sun is going down and those dratted mosquitoes will be out to eat you alive. Besides, supper will be served soon. I will join you at the table in half an hour. Jack, Tom, your clothes are in your rooms ready for you."

Both boys replied, "Thank you sir."

Before going off to their rooms, Jasper showed them where the dining room was. It was like something from an interior design magazine, dark highly polished furniture, chairs and sideboards all laid out with place settings of fine china and silverware.

The boys had changed into their own clothes and were in Tom's room chatting when a dinner gong sounded. Without hesitation they made their way down to the dining room where Gabriel directed them to the table, sat them down and laid pristine white napkins on their laps. It seemed as if much of their recent adventure had been spent in front of some sort of meal served on board a rough ship, with rough men and well, the food was pretty rough too. But this was all very grand. Sir James entered with Jasper and Kate and took their seats.

"Well gentlemen, I hope you are hungry, we have something special tonight." Sir Jasper was smiling.

Jack and Tom smiled back but they'd had too many 'special' meals in the past week or so and hoped this wouldn't be 'too' special.

Gabriel poured wine for Sir James and Jasper and more of the lime juice concoction for the boys and Kate. A maid came in with a large silver tureen which she set down on one of the sideboards. From this she ladled soup into five bowls and Gabriel served them to the awaiting diners. The liquid was green and looked like some sort of vegetable soup.

"You may start," Sir James' spoon was on the way to his mouth with Jasper close behind him.

Jack and Tom took a spoonful. It was okay. There was something familiar about it.

"It's avocado," said Jasper. "Do you know it?"

"Yes," responded Tom, "but I've never had avocado soup before, only a raw avocado in a salad. How about you Jack?"

"Same here, it is really good though."

Sir James finished his soup and looked up. "Young gentlemen, let us to business. I have arranged a crew for my sloop for tomorrow. My carriage will take you to the port from whence you will sail at ten of the clock and will be transported to Pigeon Island. My men are trustworthy and will carry you safe. Is that to your satisfaction?"

The boys thanked Sir James profusely.

"Now then, I want to hear this fantastic tale of yours. Jasper has given me some of it and it sounds somewhat, err… exaggerated? Pray tell me, from start to finish, if you please."

Jack started their story from the moment they climbed into their skiff up to the point where they were captured and taken aboard The Pelican. Tom continued then, describing life aboard the ship up to and including the battle with the Spaniards.

Sir James interrupted as the next course was brought in, "Excuse me gentlemen. Here is the surprise, the wonderful fish you caught today. Well done."

The fish was cut into portions and cooked in some kind of sauce. It was very good. Sir James complimented the three fishermen once again on their fishing prowess. The boys smiled modestly, thanking him.

This was followed by roast beef with roast potatoes and a green vegetable which might have been spinach. Sir James suggested they eat this and the boys could continue their story afterwards. They made small talk in between mouthfuls, with Kate describing her very boring existence, locked up in a cabin on the pirate ship with nothing to do apart from looking forward to a walk on deck each evening.

The main course was followed by dried fruit which had been soaked in a sort of syrup, accompanied by some decent cheese.

Sir James indicated the boys could continue with describing their adventures. "Right then my young gentlemen, pray carry on with your story. I find it fascinating."

Tom nodded to Jack suggesting he should finish relating their adventure and bring Sir James up to when they had arrived at the plantation. The rest, Sir James knew because he had been there.

When the boys had finished, Sir James said, "Well, I don't know what to believe about you both coming from the twenty-first century but I cannot doubt your sincerity. Wherever and whenever you are from, you are here now and I will be delighted to set you on your journey home. Gabriel will call you at dawn and you can be on your way."

"Thank you," both boys responded. They were attempting to stifle yawns, it had been a long and eventful day and they were completely worn out. Sir James noticing this, suggested they went to their beds so they could be up bright and early the next day. There was no argument from Jack and Tom. They gave their goodnights to Sir James, Jasper and Kate and went upstairs.

On the way to their rooms, Jack expressed his fears. "I'm excited to be setting off to Pigeon Island, Tom. But worried something will go wrong. The thought of being trapped in this century well… is absolutely terrifying."

"I feel exactly the same, Jack. Let us just hope for the best and after what we've been through, this might be the easy bit."

Once inside their rooms, both boys just collapsed onto their beds and didn't bother to undress. They wanted to jump straight out and start the journey home.

Sleep came almost immediately, but it was a restless sleep. It was interrupted with them both tossing and turning, having dreams that woke them with a start, then dropping off again. The journey home pervaded their thoughts and they were awake when Gabriel knocked on their doors.

"Thank you Gabriel," called Tom, promptly followed by the thanks from Jack. Meeting on the landing they descended the stairs and entered the dining room where Jasper was, up and dressed and eating some of the dried fruit and bread that they'd had last evening.

"Morning, Jack, Tom. I trust you slept well?"

Not wanting to even think about an awful night's sleep they just answered that they had; and helped themselves to some breakfast. Their anticipation and excitement was palpable. The fruit tasted like cardboard such was their apprehension but they washed it down with gulps of water. Food was the last thing on their minds. They were inwardly trembling.

Sir James strode in. "Right my lads! If you are ready, my carriage is waiting in the drive." He turned and headed for the front doors.

Jack, Tom and Jasper stood immediately and followed Sir James. Reaching the entrance hall they could see a black carriage, four horses in front of it and a driver sitting high up at the top. Gabriel appeared from the other side of the carriage and held opened the door. There was a cantilevered step below the door to help them from ground level to the inside of the coach. Inside they could see leather covered bench seats on each side of the coach.

"Well Jack and Tom. It has been my pleasure meeting you both. Tom, your shooting was excellent and very well timed thank you once again for saving my life."

Tom looked down, blushing slightly. "Thank you, Sir James, thank you for everything."

Jack joined in. "Yes, sir. Thank goodness we met Jasper or we wouldn't be in a position to even attempt to get home. Thank you for welcoming us into your home and for giving us the use of your sloop."

"Think nothing of it boys! Have a good journey and safe home. God speed." Sir James shook the boy's hands warmly.

"Wait! Don't go yet!" a voice came from inside the hallway, then Kate appeared and ran down the front steps and hugged the boys. Addressing Jack and Tom, she said, "Good luck, I hope you get home safely. I'm sure you have had an adventure too many. Have a safe and peaceful journey."

"Thank you Kate, it's been a pleasure knowing you," Jack was pleased to be leaving but sorry to lose his friends.

"Yes, thank you Kate," said Tom. "Please take care of yourself. Goodbye." He wasn't sure what else to say but he thought it was a sort of grown up way to leave. The three boys climbed into the carriage and as they sat down, Gabriel smiled, said goodbye and closed the door. The driver slapped the reins gently onto the horses backs and shouted, "On!" and the carriage lurched and settled into a bouncing, rolling, forward motion. The sun was coming up and the sky was a myriad of colours, with countless shades of red, pink and gold, the day was gradually lightening and after a few minutes the boys could see the slope of Spy Glass Hill that they had run down only yesterday. It seemed like a week ago.

The journey to the docks was uneventful, none of them said much. The anticipation of what was ahead filled Jack and Tom with a mixture of hope and trepidation. So much had gone wrong, hopefully, this part of their adventure would go right. Jasper, watching Jack and Tom, felt for them and guessed how they were feeling. Arriving at the docks they drove past the end of the street where Will Hardcastle lived, yet another memory of their ongoing nightmare. The carriage continued along the quay and drew to a stop beside a boat, which at about fifty or sixty feet long, was quite small in comparison to the ships they had been on recently. It was like a large sailing yacht with a single large mast in the middle with a sail in front of it and another behind. A group of sailors stood on deck staring at the carriage.

Jasper opened the door and got out onto the quay. Jack and Tom jumped out and followed Jasper down the gangplank and onto the deck. Looking up the dock, ahead they could see The Pelican and The San Francisco tied up at the dock. They automatically dropped their gaze as if doing so might stop them being seen by El Conde.

A tall man wearing what looked like an old-fashioned striped nightcap on his head stepped forward and shook Jasper's hand. Jasper introduced Jack and Tom. "This is Captain Holbrook, master of my father's sloop, The Sussex Oak. Captain, this is Jack Andrews and Tom Williams."

Captain Holbrook shook the boy's hands with vigour, almost crushing them. "Pleased to meet you both, I'm taking you lads to Pigeon Island. Can't think what you want in that god forsaken place but I'm happy to oblige Sir James. Should take us less than two days sailing. Makes a change from running sugar to Virginia. Welcome aboard."

He turned to a crewman nearby. "Simon, show these lads down below and give them a cabin."

"Aye aye Cap'n. Come with me young sirs."

It was evident that this was a working ship but everything was so neat and clean, quite unlike The Pelican. Any visible brass was polished to a high shine, the decks were pretty much spotless and the crew were all dressed in a uniform. Below deck were four cabins, all well appointed, tidy and ready for Sir James and his guests. Jack and Tom were shown into a cabin which had two bunks, narrow but adequate, made up with sheets and blankets. Jasper appeared to have the main cabin which was no doubt his father's. Outside they could hear some shouting and they felt the boat move.

Having seen their cabins, Jasper suggested they went up on deck. They were moving, very slowly, but moving, the boys heaved a sigh of relief and they grinned at each other. They watched as the crew of two rowing boats hauled on their oars to get the sloop out into open water where they could drop the sails, catch the wind and get moving.

Tom turned to Jasper and said, "Jasper, I notice as we came on board there are very few gun ports on this boat. Aren't we at risk from much bigger pirate ships?"

"Yes, as far as firepower is concerned, but the advantage of a boat like this is that it is much faster than larger ships. We can outrun them."

"Hmmm, let's hope we don't have to prove you right." He smiled, but like Jack, they'd had enough of pirates, soldiers, skirmishes and sea battles.

Once out at sea away from the port, the rowing boats and crews were brought back on board, the large triangular sails were opened to the fresh breeze and they began flashing over the waves. The sun was well up in the sky and the hot sun burned down. They were sailing west which offered blue sky right to the horizon. Behind them to the east was a vast mass of grey and black cloud.

"I reckon we're in for a storm." Captain Holbrook was assessing the cloud mass to the east. "Might pass us by, hope so anyway."

The boys looked at each other but didn't say anything. They surely couldn't have another obstacle put in their way. They were desperate to get home, this was surely the last step before getting back through what they had begun to think of as the time cave.

***

The day dragged on, they spent most of their time on deck, telling an incredulous Jasper about the twenty-first century. His understanding of television, computers, cars, aeroplanes and space travel was, the boys supposed, as difficult as theirs would be if an alien from a technologically advanced planet came to talk to them. They ate lunch and supper in the small but very posh dining room next to Sir James' cabin. The food was fresh and good because it was the first day out. Later on in a journey the use of the preserved meats such as they had in their pirate experience would probably become staple fare.

As darkness gradually fell, out on deck, everyone was looking at the mass of black clouds catching them up. By the time they turned into their bunks the wind had picked up and the boat was riding bigger and bigger waves. Someone had lit lanterns which swung from hooks in the ceiling beams. Lying on their beds fully clothed, Jack expressed his fears of what he had been thinking all day. "I hope this isn't a hurricane, Tom."

They knew about hurricanes in this part of the world. TV weather broadcasts showed the development of hurricanes from the time they were designated as 'tropical storms', through to the time their wind speeds had increased to hurricane force which was sustained winds of over seventy miles per hour. The broadcasts plotted the hurricane's course and where they were likely to hit land. At this point the boys would rather have been on land.

"I've been thinking the same, Jack. It's a bit rough out there now. I'm starting to feel a bit queasy."

As the night wore on, the weather got worse. The boat was being tossed about, rising up at the bow at what seemed a ridiculous angle then plummeting nose first into the trough between waves with the rear of the boat pitched up. Both boys were hanging on for grim death while alternatively vomiting into a wooden bucket. It was not only terrifying but being seasick compounded the problem. Suddenly, there was a clattering of feet outside their cabin and the door was flung open. It was Jasper, looking very serious.

"The captain is heading for a remote island, Santa Inez, which lies thirty miles directly to the east of Pigeon Island, to get on the lee side of it to shelter from the storm. It's not too far and it is probably our only hope." That said, he shut the cabin door and the boys barely heard his footsteps receding above the noise of the storm.

Moments later, Tom cried out, "Jack! Look! There's water coming under the door. We must be sinking!"

Jack looked at the water running into the cabin. "I think it's probably from the waves breaking on the deck, it's ok. Well… I hope so!"

The sloop was being tossed around like a cork. The noise of the wind and crashing sea was now deafening and when Jack or Tom spoke, they had to shout to be heard. They had wedged themselves in a corner between a large chest of drawers which was obviously fixed to the wall or floor or both, because it didn't move, and an outside wall. The bucket was between them, vomit slopping around inside. They jumped in terror as the cabin window smashed as a huge wave crashed into the cabin. In a few moments the cabin had six inches of water on the floor, with more coming in every time a wave hit them.

"Let's get out of here, now!" Tom was on his feet and hauling up Jack by his arm.

They were flung around the cabin as the boat tossed and heaved. With a struggle they made it to the door and got out into the small corridor which led to the steps up to the deck. Waves were now crashing down the stairs. The boys were soaked as they made it to the deck. Just as they stepped onto the deck a huge gust of wind hit the sloop which tipped it violently sideways. Jack and Tom were flung to the bulwark, the three-foot-high wooden wall which surrounded the deck where they desperately tried to hold on. A second later, a massive wave washed over the deck and threw them overboard.

Panic stricken, Jack came to the surface fighting for breath. It was pitch dark and he couldn't see anything, not even the sloop. Swimming for his life, trying to stay afloat, waves broke over him and he was swallowing water. "This is it he thought. I'm going to drown." For what seemed an eternity he was thrown around by the sea, he was tiring fast.

Suddenly, the noise of the crashing sea changed to a roaring sound, he was picked up and carried for some distance, dropped, then carried again. Hope sprang in him, this felt like waves near a beach. A huge wave picked him up again and carried him with enormous force. His feet struck the seabed and he was flung around by breaking waves as if he were inside a washing machine. In a flash, Jack was upside down underwater being pummelled by the pressure of the waves. Just when he thought he would pass out from lack of oxygen he surfaced and was hurled like a rag doll onto solid ground. He was on a beach! He had to find the strength to get up the beach because he knew these waves might suck him back into the sea. Crawling on all fours he made his way up the beach, eventually finding his feet and getting to a slope which felt like a sand dune. He made his way up to a level part of the dune and he lay down, utterly exhausted and devastated.

"What now? Where was Tom?" This was just awful, more than a lifetime's horrors all happening in just a week or so. He would never get home. Jack began to sob but soon drifted into a deep dreamless sleep, temporarily safe from his anguish.

Eight

"Hey, wake up!"

Jack was startled awake. He found it difficult to open his eyes without sand scratching them. He rubbed them with the bottom of his tee shirt. He thought he had been dreaming. It was daylight and realisation of last night came back with a bang. The wind was gusting but was obviously dying off from the storm or hurricane or whatever it was.

"Come on, Jack!" It was Tom, he was safe too. Jack leapt up and hugged Tom, a smile running from ear to ear.

"What? How? Did you get washed ashore like me?"

"Stupid question, Jack. I'm here aren't I? It was a close run thing though. I thought I was a goner."

"Well, I'm delighted you're here. But where are we and what happened to the Sussex Oak? Did they all drown? What happened to Jasper?" Jack was upset.

"It doesn't look good. There's no sign of them and that was a horrendous storm, thank goodness it's over."

Jack responded, "It's just too awful to think about. There's nothing we can do except think about where we are and what we're going to do. Let's take a look around the beach and see if we can find anyone else. We also need to find water to drink."

They set off. The coastline of what they assumed was the island of Santa Inez, where Captain Holbrook was going to shelter, was straight for about half a mile then disappeared around a corner. The beach was fine soft white sand. The inner island was a low hill, heavily wooded with some large palm and tropical trees. They soon started discovering bits of wood, two small empty barrels and boxes which were scattered along the beach, obviously having been washed off the sloop. As they walked, they made piles of everything they could carry or drag together, higher up the beach. Carrying boxes and crates between them, they had to leave some of the heavier ones. They decided to return to the piles they had made when they had finished their search, in case there was anything they could use to survive. They walked to the point at which the beachline turned. They could see the other side of the island as it narrowed to almost a point at the end. Walking across to the other side they began their search along the northern side.

"What's that? Is it a body?" Tom called out and pointed at a low mound on the beach about a hundred yards ahead.

They ran towards it. It was evident as they approached it wasn't a body. Reaching it, they were surprised to find that it was a rolled up sail. Perhaps a spare that had been on deck and washed overboard.

"What on earth has happened to that boat?" Tom gazed out to sea. "Poor old Jasper. He was our friend."

"Yes, I know we were leaving him but I never expected to leave him like this." Jack felt tears prickle his eyes. This was as much for their own situation as for Jasper so he felt a bit guilty, thinking of himself when he was alive but Jasper was possibly dead.

He glanced further along the beach at the base of a group of trees. "Tom! Is that what I think it is?" Jack began running in the direction of the trees.

"Yes! Yes!" Tom could see now, it was one of the rowing boats from the sloop.

They were overjoyed. Reaching the boat they inspected it for damage. It was the right way up and had been washed up onto the beach and came to a stop between a group of palm trees. The bow was facing the sea.

"This could be our means of escape Jack. Maybe we could rig a mast onto it and use the sail we found to create a sailing boat? Jasper said that Pigeon Island is thirty miles to the west of here. It's the best plan we've got."

"I agree, but we've got to move it back to the water, This is going to be a very heavy boat. We're going to have to cut the sail down to fit the size of our boat. First things first. I think we should carry on around the island and see what else we can find."

"Okay, let's go."

They had walked about another hundred yards when they came across a stream which emptied onto the beach and almost disappeared into the sand, soaking the beach right down to the sea. Following it inland for a hundred yards they could see that its source was a further up the hill. As it got closer to the sea, it became a small torrent tumbling down the hillside over a rocky bed towards the beach.

"Fantastic! A water supply. We'll be okay Tom. We'll need to get some containers to collect it." The boys were delighted.

"Maybe we should make a camp nearby," Tom suggested. "We'll have a water supply and we'll be close to the rowing boat, it makes sense."

"Good idea."

After completing the circuit of the island they found nothing else of apparent value other than a length of fairly thin rope about ten yards long still attached to a belaying pin. They took it with them to the first pile of flotsam. There were two large wooden chests. These were too heavy to move so had to be opened in situ. The lids were held shut by a long iron rod going through metal loops. Sliding the rod out of the first one they opened the chest. They couldn't believe their luck. Although the box was half full of water, inside were three large axes, two hammers and two large machete type knives. Inside some waxed canvas were dozens of primitive iron nails.

"Yes! What a great find! We're having a bit of luck." Tom was elated.

"Let's open the other chests and see if we're as lucky." Jack couldn't believe their luck would continue.

Opening the second chest they had another exciting find. Rope and pulleys. The boys knew about pulleys from living near a fishing port at home and they had also learned in maths lessons at school, about how they effectively reduced the effort required to lift or move something.

"We should be able to use these to lift heavy items or if we build a shelter with trees we cut down. Maybe even get the rowing boat into the water." Jack's brain was whirring like a computer.

They opened the remaining boxes and crates. Some of them had nothing but unrecognisable tools or bracket-like pieces of iron, obviously something to do with eighteenth century ships. One small box had several smallish but sharp knives and some fishing line and hooks, an almost priceless find which would help them catch food. Another important find was a Tinder Box. This was something they had seen sailors using to get some flame to light their pipes. It was a a small steel container, in the shape of a cylinder, containing flint and fibrous dry cloth or other fine material which ignited easily and used together to help light a fire. Attached to the cylinder was a oval shaped piece of thin steel which was held over some of the dry material and then struck against the flint to cause a spark. The spark lit the material.

Probably the most valuable find for the immediate future was a box with what they could only describe as hardtack biscuits and another with a salt pork joint wrapped in a sort of muslin material caked with salt. At least they had some food. The bungs in the two small barrels were missing and were empty apart from some seawater sploshing around inside but they smelled very strongly of rum.

"We can use these for water but we're going to have to try to wash the smell of rum out of them." Tom turned his nose up at the overpowering smell of the strong spirit.

"Right Jack, we should get everything around to the other side of the island as near as possible to the stream and make a camp. It's also close to the boat."

They worked for the rest of the day, stopping for a few hardtack biscuits and several drinks from the stream. Carrying boxes and everything they felt would be of use, to a position about twenty yards to one side of the stream. Retrieving the sail was hard work. It was large and extremely heavy so they had to open it out to drag it which made it easier. Once back near their campsite, they tied it between four trees about four feet from the ground as a shelter for the night. The sail was so large it hung down on each side like a tent.

Jack looked at their home for the night. "Hmm… I think we ought to make something a bit more permanent than this. We can do it tomorrow."

Tom sounded a little sceptical. "Well let's hope we won't need a shelter for too long. It will do for a while, it's warm enough during the day and night but we'll need shelter if it rains. I think we should use the sail as a sail. We ought to get that boat closer to the water and then see if we can get a mast made and securely fitted."

"I agree with that but if we don't get a shelter made it could be pretty miserable if it rains every day. It's a massive piece of canvas so we will easily have enough left over for a sail after we've made a shelter."

***

As darkness fell, the sky was an amazing array of colours as the sun set. Sitting down outside the shelter, they decided to eat. Unwrapping the salt pork, Jack cut off a decent slice for each of them to eat with a couple of biscuits. Not the best supper but they were used to sailor's food, and it was better than nothing. They had to walk to the stream and put their faces in and drink like animals as they had nothing to use as cups.

"Tomorrow we should try to achieve several major things," Jack had his serious voice on. "One, try to get the longboat up the water's edge using the pulleys. Then, cut a log suitable for a mast and mount it and a sail onto the boat. Two, build a shelter. Three, get a baited fishing line in the water to catch some fish. And Four, before dark, see if we can light a fire using the tinder box. If we can achieve that we will be able to cook any fish we might have caught."

"Yeah, good thinking. Catching fish might be tricky but we should persist. This pork will run out in a few days."

"Well, I'd rather hoped we wouldn't be here for too long. I hoped we would be at home." Jack paused for a moment, "Oh yes, we should collect coconuts and get at the liquid and flesh inside too."

"Good thinking Robinson Crusoe."

The wind had dropped to almost nothing, the storm had well and truly passed, it was a warm tropical night. The boys decided to turn in and lay down under the sail that was their temporary home. The sand was soft and fine but still uncomfortable to sleep on. In spite of that, they slept and spent a reasonable night, waking occasionally but drifting off again.

***

As dawn broke, Tom woke first and shook Jack. He woke with a start, "What's up!"

"Nothing you twit, time to get up and get some work done."

"Oh, right. I was dreaming we were in Sennac and telling my dad that I'd had a dream about being kidnapped by pirates and being shipwrecked. Then I wake up to find that it isn't a dream."

"Okay, number one priority, let's get the boat closer to the water from where we can launch it. Our main priority is getting to Pigeon Island. If we can't do that, we're in trouble."

"Yes, Jack, Let's get on with it."

Eating two hardtack biscuits each and taking a drink from the stream they organised themselves for their task. Picking up as much rope as they could carry along with three pulleys, which were heavy, they set off to the boat which was only a few hundred yards along the beach. Arriving at the boat they took stock of the situation. The boat had been pushed about twenty yards up the beach where it had come to a halt against a palm tree. There were several palm trees and two of them were ten yards closer to the sea in an almost direct line to the boat. This was sheer good fortune. They could use these trees as an anchor point for the pulleys.

After some discussion about the technology required to make the pulleys work and how best to use them. They tied a pulley to one of the trees. The second pulley was attached to the bow of the boat. Tying one end of a rope to the tree parallel to the one with the first pulley they threaded it through the pulley attached to the boat, then through the other pulley. Taking the loose end and standing near the boat they began to heave. Breaking into a sweat with the effort, they strained and pulled. The boat didn't move an inch. They collapsed, feeling rather sorry for themselves.

"We can do this! Come on Tom, think!"

"Yes, I've got it. We can roll it on logs!"

"Ah, yes. But we need to lift it to get the logs under it."

"We can move the pulley system to these trees and lift it off the sand, high enough to get a couple of logs under the bow to give it a start."

"Great idea, Tom!" Jack's enthusiasm was back.

Tom smiled, "Yes, let's cut some logs."

They went back to their camp, picked up an axe and a machete each and climbed up the slope into the trees. Sourcing young trees about four inches in diameter they made short work of them. Cutting them down with an axe and trimming them to about five feet long, it took about an hour or so to collect ten logs, which were small enough for the boys to manage in several trips.

The next stage was to rearrange the pulley system on the trees adjacent to the boat. This task didn't take too long except they could not get the pulleys very high up the trees without standing on the sides of the boat. Task completed, they hauled on the rope. Because they were only lifting the front of the boat they managed to get it a foot or so out of the sand. Tying off the loose end of the rope they then put three logs under the front end of the keel of the boat. Untying the rope they eased the boat down onto the logs.

The sun was well up in the sky and blazed down with an intensity. The boys were soaked with sweat from their exertions. They couldn't stop though. Taking down the two pulleys they put them back on the forward trees, in the same configuration as they'd had earlier. When all was ready, using all their strength, they hauled again on the rope.

"It's moving!" cried Jack. They were elated as the boat moved a couple of feet.

"Right, stop pulling Jack. Let's get more logs underneath." The first three logs were now back towards the middle of the keel, the bow still raised off the beach. The boys placed three more logs underneath and took up the rope again.

"Okay, heave!" Jack sounded like a tug-of-war boss. The boat eased forward again another short distance. It didn't take them long to complete the job of moving the boat into position next to the two forward trees only ten yards from the sea. Hauling the boat forward, stopping, placing logs underneath and pulling again. As the boat went over the first, then subsequent logs, these were picked up and used at the front again. When they were done, they fell onto the sand, really pleased with themselves. Laughing with pleasure and relief, they knew that when they had contrived a mast and sail they could use the log system, even without the pulleys, to push the boat down the slight slope of the beach into the sea.

The sun was almost at its zenith, they had been working for five or six hours but still had plenty to do.

"What do you think about looking for a tree suitable for a mast?" Tom lay on the sand, his face turned towards Jack.

"Yep. Let's go. Enough of this lazing around. We've got homes to go to!" A nagging doubt still played on their minds that this might be wishful thinking. Taking their axes and machetes once again, they made their way into the trees.

"How big do you reckon we should make the mast? That sail is massive, we'll need to cut it down." Tom was thinking ahead.

"I reckon about the same diameter as those rolling logs we cut and ten feet tall?"

After a short search, Jack called out to Tom. "Over here, I think this will do."

Tom made his way through some scrubby undergrowth to where Jack was and looked at the tree. It was currently about twenty feet tall, and looked about the right thickness.

"We'll chop it down, cut it to the right length then trim the branches off. I haven't a clue how we're going to secure this to the boat. Have you?"

Tom pondered a moment, "No, not really but we'll have to come up with something or the whole exercise is pointless."

Standing on each side of the tree, the boys attacked it with their axes. Tom first, followed by Jack. They hadn't done anything like this before and if it it had been a larger tree they could have been in peril of it falling on them but energy overtook skill and the tree soon began to crack and lean as the upper weight began tell.

"Okay Tom, you stop, stand back and I reckon a few more lumps out of this side will do the trick." Tom stepped away as Jack chopped another half dozen times, chips of wood leaping out of the widening gap. The tree gave a long creaking and cracking noise and fell towards them. Leaping to one side, the boys were safe but had learned something from their lumberjack efforts.

Jack offered his observations. "I think if we do this again we should chop to about half way on one side then chop the other side so in theory it should fall the way we want it to."

"Yeah. I think you're right. That was a bit dangerous." Looking at the fallen tree, Tom said, "Do you want to pace out about ten feet and start chopping it off to length?"

Jack obliged while Tom sat on the damp ground and looked on. Jack stopped after several minutes of hard chopping, arms aching from the effort. They were hot, weary, hungry and thirsty and the constant worry of getting home sapped energy too. They could not stop though. The burning desire to get out of their situation drove them on. Tom took over until the tree was cut through and at the required length. Using the axes and machetes they trimmed off the branches until the fallen tree was a log, soon to be a mast. Or so they hoped.

Without a word between them, they picked up an end of the log each and hoisted it onto their shoulders. Axes in their other hands and machetes stuck through their belts they set off back to the beach. The log wasn't overly heavy so it they didn't find it too difficult a task to carry it back. Once at the boat they dropped everything and collapsed onto the sand. At least part of the plan for the day was coming together.

"Fancy a quick swim to wash off the sweat Tom?"

"I was just thinking the same."

The boys stripped off to their boxer shorts and ran the few yards and plunged into the warm Caribbean Sea. It was wonderful. This side of the island had a reef about two hundred yards offshore. The sea had calmed and the water was crystal clear, the only waves were breaking on the reef itself which acted like a barrier creating what was almost like a lake inside it. Fish of every shape and size with all the colours of the rainbow darted around in the shallow water.

"We ought to get a line with a baited hook in the water, Jack. I reckon we might get lucky. I've never gutted and prepared a fish for cooking but we've seen enough fishermen at home do it so I think we could get by. What do you think?"

"Good idea. I'm starved. Let's go and have a slice of salt pork with a biscuit and get the fishing tackle out. We could try baiting the hook with a piece of salt pork."

"Hmm… Won't it be too salty for the fish to be attracted?"

"Tom, they live in salty water. I don't think they would notice!"

Tom laughed, "Ahh… yes, you might have a point there."

Arriving back at their camp, they went and drank deeply from the stream and washed the sea water out of their hair because they had discovered it dried caked with salt which ran into their eyes when they sweated. Tom unwrapped the salt pork and cut off a slice for each of them. Eaten with the dry hardtack biscuits it was not really a meal to savour but was all they had. They munched away looking out to sea, pondering the situation. Jack finished his last bite of pork, stood up and walked towards a group of palm trees a hundred yards along the beach.

"What are you doing?" Tom asked.

"Come on, let's go and collect some fallen coconuts that are lying around."

Jack and Tom really had not stopped working since they woke up and so hadn't had a chance to collect some of these precious fruits. Breaking into a trot, Tom caught up with Jack and they quickly made it to the trees.

"Yes!" Tom cried out. "Look Jack, here's a few!"

Scattered around the base of the tree were four coconuts lying in the sand. Unlike when buying them at home, these had the outer husk covering the shell. A tough outer layer over the thick, dense fibre underneath, which would have to be cut off before they could get at the inner shell and the milk and flesh. Looking up they could see clusters of the fruit still attached to the top of the trees, ten yards above their heads. The trees, too high and too smooth to climb, the boys knew that these coconuts would remain there until nature caused them to drop.

"We'll take these back and see if we can chop through the husk to get at the milk and flesh inside."

Picking up two coconuts each they walked back to the camp. They had seen people in films and nature programmes on TV chopping the tops off coconuts with machetes. Putting one of them on its side into a hollow in the sand, Jack took one of the machetes and gave the coconut a mighty whack. The blade cut into the outer husk making a long deep cut.

"Ahh, this may take a while," said Jack without enthusiasm.

However, three or four chops later the top of the inner hard shell was exposed. The top of the shell exposed three small indentations that his Dad told him were called 'eyes.' Taking the small knife they used for cutting the pork, Jack was soon through two of the eyes and offered the coconut to Tom.

"Here Tom, you go first. Have a swig."

Tom took the coconut, held it to his mouth and tipped back his head.

"Oh my goodness! That's the best thing ever. It's delicious and amazingly cool. You have some."

Jack had a drink and expressed the same sentiments, adding, "We'll have to get a store of these, we can take some with us if we can manage to get our boat underway. When we've got some time we'll go on a coconut hunt."

Finishing off the small amount of coconut milk with a couple more swigs each, which wasn't really milk at all, but good all the same, they decided to make drinking cups of the inner, hard shells. Taking a second coconut, Jack chopped through to the inner shell and they shared the delicious fluid from that one too.

Laying the coconuts on their sides Jack first chopped across the top, cutting across the inner shell so there was an opening large enough to pour liquid into and drink from when the outer husk was removed. He then hacked at the outer husk, trying very hard not to shatter the inner shell. After ten minutes or so, he achieved their objective. Very pleased with themselves, they took their new drinking vessels to the stream and filled them. With the coconut flesh still inside the inner shells the water was slightly flavoured but the cups worked.

"I think we should get the coconut flesh out because it might rot, besides, its fresh fruit and is good for us, I suppose," said Tom. He picked up a smaller knife and began cutting away at it.

Jack followed suit, both the boys pulling out bits of the soft sweet flesh which they greedily stuffed into their mouths. They were finished in no time as they had never had such fresh coconuts and didn't realise the flesh was soft, unlike the dried, chewy stuff they got at home. Happy with their new food and drink supply, they agreed they should find more when they had finished their other objectives.

"Right, what shall we do next Tom?"

"Well, I think we should leave the boat for now and see if we can get some kind of shelter built for tonight, I think it looks like rain. That will give us all of tomorrow to try to get a sail on the boat."

"Agreed, but let's throw a line and baited hook into the water and see what happens. We can tie the line to one of those forward trees."

Opening the box, Tom retrieved the fishing line which was wound around a wooden frame about six inches square. The corners of the frame protruded out about an inch from the right angle so it looked a bit like a hash symbol on a mobile phone keyboard. These protrusions were designed to keep the line from unravelling. Finding the end of the line he unwound about a foot or so and choosing a medium sized hook, he tied it on. The line was made of a fine, hair-like material plaited together. It looked and felt like the hair from a horse's tail.

Tom put a half inch piece of pork on the hook and walked towards the sea while Jack unwound the line. Wading into the water he stopped, "Jack, we need a forked stick to hold the line up so it dangles into the water."

"Yep, you're right. Just hang on and I'll be back in a flash." Jack dropped the line and raced into the trees to where they had chopped the log for their mast. A few moments later he was running back with a branch they had lopped off the log. It was about four feet long and forked at the end. Stopping at the camp, using a machete, he quickly trimmed the branch, leaving a six-inch fork at the top and then cut a sharp point at the bottom.

Joining Tom at the water's edge together they pushed the sharp stick into the soft sand with the 'V' of the top end about two feet above the surface of the water. Tying a small piece of wood above the hook to act as a float, Jack then unwound enough line to tie to one of the large palm trees which were near the water's edge. Tom then hung the baited hook over the 'V' of the stick and dangled it about a foot in the water.

"Primitive but it might work." Tom walked up the beach to Jack.

"We might be lucky. Let's build a shelter."

Jack had an idea. "Tom, before we do anything else we should wash out those small rum kegs so we can store water in them."

They walked back to camp and on Jack's suggestion, smashed the tops out of the kegs so they were open at one end. The tops were round discs of wood which although broke in half when the bashed them free they would be useful for something. Carrying a keg each, they took them to the water's edge and filled them with sea water and gave them a number of rinses, washing the insides with sand mixed with sea water. The result was fairly clean kegs with still a faint smell of rum.

Jack was concerned at the amount of time they had left before it got dark. It seemed they had so many things to do still. "We can put them in the stream and wash them with clean water. I don't think we'll get rid of the rum smell totally but it should help. Let's do that this evening."

Tom agreed and felt that they should get on now with shelter building, so before picking up their axes and machetes they discussed how they might achieve their construction plan.

"What do you think about using the slope at the back of the beach here as the rear wall. If we get some upright poles into the beach, with some horizontal support beams we can put a roof on."

"Yes, we can cut a large piece of the sail to use as a roof covering to go on top of the frame."

Jack was getting into this now. The challenge of overcoming their situation was a powerful driving force. Climbing up the slope they chose some sturdy trees for the framework. Getting to work quickly they chopped and hacked down and trimmed off the branches of a dozen or so over the next couple of hours. It was hot sweaty work but they had also brought with them their coconut shell cups topped up with water and had stood them up in a hollow, balanced against a large tree. Not a lot of water but sufficient to take the odd sip and keep their mouths from drying up. Satisfied with their work, they hoisted several of the poles onto their shoulders and carried them back to camp. A second trip completed the task and they stood contemplating the next stage.

Tom spoke up. "What do you think about digging holes to put the posts in and I'll look around to find some stones to drop in to support them. We can then fill the holes back up with sand."

"Yep, I'll go for that," replied Jack. "I'll find something to use as a shovel. I expect you will find some stones or rocks in and around the stream. In the sea too."

Tom set off to the stream to look for stones while Jack retrieved a semi-circle of wood which had been half of the circular disc of wood at the top of the small barrel. The back end of the beach was a slope, with a rocky outcrop about six feet high. They were going to use this outcrop as the back wall to the shelter. That being the case, Jack took three paces from the back wall and made a quick hollow to mark the spot for one of the upright posts. He then walked the same distance parallel with that and marked the position for the second post. He began to dig using his improvised shovel.

The sand was soft and easy to dig but being fine it kept pouring back into the hole, making Jack dig faster. Persisting, within a few minutes he had dug down about two feet which he thought would be enough. He moved on to the second position and commenced digging. Hearing Tom approaching, Jack looked up. Tom had an armful of large stones and rocks.

"Quick Jack, before I drop these, stand one of the posts in the hole and hold it straight and I'll dump them in."

Jack jumped up and quickly got a post and putting it into the hole, held it upright. Tom tipped in the stones. Jack let go and the post was reasonably stable, all he had to do now was to fill the hole around the stones with as much sand as possible.

"Right I'll collect more and if you can get the second hole dug by the time I come back with the rocks, we can both get on and finish the job."

Jack concurred, "Okay, I'll get this done in a few minutes."

After an hour or so they were well on with the shelter. The upright posts were firmly in position and they had tied cross pieces to these as the horizontal supports for the sail canvas they were putting on for the roof. Two of these ran from the top of the rocky outcrop which was the back wall of their shelter, to the upright posts. A third log went from the middle of the horizontal support which ran between the two uprights, to the top of the back wall. They had the framework tied together with some of the thinner rope. The next part of the operation was to cut enough of the canvas to cover the frame, making sure that they would have enough left to make a suitable sized sail for the boat. Laying it out on the beach it was pretty huge.

Tom looked at the canvas sail laid out in front of them. "I reckon we'll need a triangular piece of canvas about seven feet long by five feet along the bottom edge for the sail. We need to make a boom for the bottom of the sail, it will help us steer and without that the wind could tip the boat."

This knowledge came from the fact that Jack and Tom had been sailing since they were very young.

"You're right Tom. We'll have to get that sorted tomorrow when we try to get the sail rigged. Meanwhile, let's cut off what we want for the sail and we can use the rest for the roof of our shelter."

Tom held up one edge of the canvas while Jack held further along with one hand while he sawed at it with a machete. The canvas was tough but the machete was pretty sharp. Half way through, Jack's sawing arm was painful from the effort. The boys switched places and Tom took over. It took a good twenty minutes before Tom cut through the the last bit. Carrying the larger piece over to their construction, they took a side each and dragged the canvas up onto the top of the shelter frame. Once in position, Jack climbed up onto the bank that was the back wall of their new home and laid one of the cut logs along the edge of the canvas to hold it in place.

Jack jumped back down to help Tom secure the canvas to the rest of the frame. They found and chopped some thinner saplings into shorter lengths and knocked these into the sand to use as tent pegs, using a hammer from one of the boxes. Then, tying ropes to the canvas, they used these like guy ropes and secured them to the tent pegs. In a very short time they had a waterproof roof stretched out on the frame.

"Well, let's hope this is just for a temporary stay. However, it should give us shelter while we're here. We're going to need more weight on the edge of the canvas I reckon. That should keep it more secure."

A short while later they had collected enough stones and rocks to weigh the canvas down to keep it in place on the top of the rocky outcrop.

"We need to eat before it gets dark and that will be in an hour or so. Don't know about you but I'm starving. Let's check our fishing line!" Tom started down the beach.

Jack had forgotten all about it, being totally preoccupied by the afternoon's work. "Huh! We should be so lucky." He was not too optimistic.

Arriving at their fishing line, Tom walked into the water up to his knees. "Yes! We've got a fish!"

Neither of them could believe their luck. There at the end of the line, still on the hook was a dark pink fish of decent size. It had exhausted itself trying to get off the line and was barely alive as Tom removed the hook. He gave its head a sharp smack on a rock just at the water's edge. Both boys loved wildlife but this was about survival. The fish was now dead.

"Okay, Jack. We need fire to cook this thing. Let's see if you can use the tinder box and get the fire going."

"Hmm… I'll give it a go. We'll find some wood for the fire then I'll get some dry leaves and stuff for tinder. If it doesn't work, I don't fancy raw fish."

Tom agreed, "Me neither!" They went off to collect wood for a fire.

There was plenty of dead wood and branches lying around amongst the trees. Collecting a decent load, the boys piled it up and Jack pulled dry dead leaves off some of the branches along with some thin twigs. Opening the tinder box cylinder he took out a small wad of the material which he pulled it apart until the fibres were exposed and laid it on the dry leaves. He piled a few of these on top for good measure. Taking the steel oval ring he put four fingers of his right hand through it and holding the flint flat to the ground struck it sharply several times. Sparks flew but nothing happened. Jack increased his efforts. Once again, sparks flew and then to his delight the material began to burn and smoulder. He then did what he had seen the sailors do. He blew on the smouldering material until it burst into flames. The dry leaves caught quickly, followed by the twigs, they then put slightly larger pieces on which began to burn steadily. Gradually, it was a proper small bonfire.

"Err… how are we going to cook the fish?" Jack could do scrambled eggs on toast but cooking a whole fish was not part of his repertoire.

"We'll have to gut and scale it first. I've watched my dad do it, so I'm sure it can't be that difficult." Tom, carrying the fish, walked down to the water's edge with one of the small knives.

Standing in the water, he inserted the point of the knife into the underside of the fish near its tail. Pushing slightly, he ran the blade along the belly, opening it up. The fish's guts hung out, then using the blade, Tom scraped them into the sea. Kneeling down, he washed the fish with his fingers, rinsing it with seawater. He stood again, placing the fish on a rock at the water's edge, then scraped the sharp edge of the knife along the sides of the body from the tail towards the head in quick long strokes. This was de-scaling. After doing one side he turned the fish over and did the other side. Tom came back to Jack with the fish, ready to cook.

"I've got an idea, Tom. What about wrapping the fish in a large leaf and putting it onto the hot embers? I've seen that on TV documentaries."

"Yes, so have I. Good idea."

Jack jumped up and although it was now dusk, he climbed up the bank into the trees and began a search for a likely-looking leaf. Machete in hand he walked through the scrubby undergrowth looking up at trees. Spotting a low tree with huge leaves he slashed his machete at the base of the leaves. Collecting three of them he walked back the short distance to their camp.

They wrapped the fish in the leaves, a sort of triple wrapped parcel and using a stick, Jack pushed the still burning upper wood and branches to one side, exposing red hot coals. Tom then put the fish parcel into the embers.

"How long do you reckon?" he asked.

Jack pondered, "Hmm, no idea but not long, twenty minutes? Just thinking, I hope those leaves aren't poisonous."

"Thanks for that Jack. I don't fancy being ill or dying here when we might be close to getting home."

"We'll just have to take that chance, it would be good to get some fresh food down us. While we're waiting for it to cook, I'll chop the tops off the other two coconuts so we can have a drink of something other than water. I could really do with a coke or a lemonade or something."

Tom nodded and stared wistfully into the fire. He seemed to snap out of his trance after a few moments and said to Jack, "What are we going to use for plates?"

Jack thought for a while, glancing around their quickly darkening camp. "I know, we can use the keg lids we smashed in. They're covered in sand but I'll wash them in the stream."

Jack picked up the slightly damaged lids and took them to the stream and gave them a good wash. Returning they sat while willing the time to go by so they could see what their fish was like.

Jack checked his watch. "Okay chef, let's check the fish."

Tom used a stick to pull the fish parcel out of the fire. The leaves were smouldering and looked charred. Sliding it onto one of the keg lids he opened the parcel, yelping now and again as he singed his fingers.

"Ouch! This is hot."

"Well done Einstein, it's been in a fire." Jack smiled.

"It will have to cool off a bit so I can hold it and cut it down the back bone to share it out. I'll put it to one side for a few minutes. Shall we sort out those coconuts?"

Jack got cracking with his trusty machete and chopped off the tops then passed one of them to Tom, he then picked up his. They both drank deeply, barely stopping for a breath. They both exclaimed their pleasure with words like "Wow!" and "Wonderful!"

"We can chop them open later to get at the flesh for dessert." Jack wiped his mouth with the back of his hand as he spoke.

Testing the fish with a finger for temperature Tom set it on the keg lid. He then took his knife and opened up the fish to expose the backbone. He gently cut through along one side of the backbone so the fish ended up in two halves. He pushed half of it onto the other keg lid and passed it to Jack.

The sun had gone but light from the fire showed the flesh of the fish as a rosy pink. Picking the meat off the bones they stuffed the fish into their mouths with their fingers.

Occasionally a bone or two had to be retrieved and thrown out but it didn't deter them. It was good.

Opening the box with the hardtack biscuits they had two each to fill their bellies. They had found that these biscuits, although tasteless and as the clue was in their name, they were rather hard, they did seem to swell in their stomachs and make them feel full. After their main course, Jack attacked the coconuts with his machete and quickly got to the inner shells. They literally woofed down the coconut flesh. Having finished their suppers they both felt a wave of tiredness sweep over them. They had worked hard all day and were very weary. The fire was just a few glowing embers when they crawled into the new shelter. The sky had cleared of the heavy threatening clouds and the threat of rain had gone. A light warm wind rustled the canvas shelter. The situation would have been idyllic in any other circumstances other than the one the boys found themselves in.

Lying side by side on their backs, hands behind heads, Tom said, "We should bait the fishing line first thing. We might catch something again."

"Good idea. We might get the sail done on the boat tomorrow. Before we leave, perhaps we should try to catch several fish, cook them and try to preserve them somehow, we may need food for the journey. Who knows, we might get lost. Hate to say it, but sailing due west may not be good enough. We can also collect coconuts and fill the kegs with water."

Tom didn't reply, he was fast asleep.

Nine

Breaking dawn saw both boys on their feet and stretching, sand fell off them as they moved. The sand was hard and uncomfortable but they had slept without waking. They had achieved a lot the day before. Today was the big day for trying to get a sail rigged on the rowing boat. As suggested the previous evening, Tom got on with setting up the fishing line. He took some pork as bait and after a few minutes got the fishing line back in the water.

Returning, to camp, Tom joined Jack in some breakfast of salt pork and hardtack biscuits. They were edgy and ate standing up, eager to get on with what they hoped was the last part of their journey. The fear of not successfully completing it to enable them to get home was a constant fear. Drinking a coconut shell full of water to wash down breakfast, they walked to the boat and stood looking at the inside and tried to figure out how to attach a mast which would take the stress and strain of a sail. Inside were the four lateral wooden boards across the width of the boat. The boards were in fact the seats used by the rowers. At the back was a seat where the tillerman sat to operate the rudder to steer. The boat was about twelve feet long and four feet wide, so it was big and heavy and needed an eight-man crew to row it.

Jack posed a question, looking at Tom. "What do you think about chopping a hole in the middle of the second board, big enough to drop our mast through then nailing some other wood around it then some ropes securing it in an upright position?"

"Yeah, right sort of idea but it's going to be difficult to get a decent hole cut in it without destroying the whole board. We've only got one go at this because the mast can only really be placed on that second board. It's very hard wood too, which will make it almost impossible trying to get through the middle with the tools we've got. I think it might be better to chop a semi-circular shaped chunk out of it, the diameter of the mast, into the edge of it, cutting up to about half way in the board, putting the mast in and then nailing another piece of wood across the board to hold it in place."

"I see what you mean. I think you're right. Let's mark it out and we'll get going."

With Jack holding the bottom of the mast on the seat board, Tom scratched a line with his knife equal to its diameter on either side of it to give a guide for the width of the piece they were going to cut out. He then scratched a line at the half way point of the board. That was the end limit of the proposed semi-circular cut. Any further and it would likely weaken the board.

"Okay, I'll go first," said Tom.

He stood behind the board and gave a chop with his machete. It bounced off making only a shallow gouge.

"Ahh, I think this is going to need an axe."

Jack ran back to the shelter picked up an axe and took it to Tom.

Tom, standing on the board, feet wide apart, the axe made it a bit easier because it was heavier; but difficult to do anything other than send large uneven chunks flying out of the board. He did however make some progress but the opening he was cutting was soon wider than the diameter of the mast.

"I'm not too worried about the width, Jack, because we can nail some wood on either side of the mast to hold it in position."

Puffing with the effort, Tom jumped out of the boat and suggested that Jack use a machete to try to trim off the edges. Jack climbed in and after a while they had a rough 'D' shaped opening in the forward edge of the board which just about reached the middle. Not quite what they wanted but might do the job once they had nailed wood around the mast.

Erecting the mast into position, the rest of morning was spent nailing wooden supports to the seat board around it. They then attached guy ropes, tied from the mast and nailed to the front and two sides of the boat to give it stability. Tugging on the mast, it seemed to be fairly secure. The next jobs were to cut the sail to size and also find a decent tree suitable to chop down and use for a boom.

Stopping for a break, they checked the fishing line and were disappointed to find the hook, bait still attached, dangling in the water.

"Hmm. Hopefully, something will take a bite this afternoon." Pessimism mixed with optimism for Jack.

Hot and sweaty, the boys had a ten minute dip in the sea to cool off and having decided to go on a coconut hunt they then wandered a few hundred yards along the beach to a group of coconut palms. There were five of the precious fruits just waiting to be picked up. They carried them back to camp between them. Jack had become the expert coconut chopper-opener and did his stuff. They were soon drinking the delicious cool sweet milk and shortly afterwards dining on the flesh. Not terribly filling but better than eating that awful salty pork. Jack volunteered to find a slim but sturdy tree suitable for a boom while Tom dragged the remaining canvas over to the boat where he estimated that the sail should be triangular, and as they had agreed, about seven feet high by and five feet wide at the bottom.

Walking back to where they'd had their fire Tom picked up a piece of burnt wood, the end of which had turned to charcoal. Using it as a marking pen, he drew out a shape just slightly larger than the size he had estimated. By the time he had finished, Jack was back with a trimmed tree trunk, about three inches in diameter, just right for the boom.

Working together, using the machetes again, following the charcoal marks, they cut the canvas into the triangular shape required for the sail. The next stage was to attach it to the mast. Using nails they nailed the bottom edge to the boom. Next, with some ingenious work they threaded rope in and out along the straight edge of the sail after poking holes in the canvas with a knife. To tie the whole thing to the top of the mast, Jack sat on Tom's shoulders while he stood on the seat board, holding onto the mast for stability. Jack tied the rope securely using the pre-cut notches at the top of the mast. After this, they tied the bottom of the sail and boom to the lower end of the mast. To finish off they attached a rope to the loose end of the boom. This would be to control the sail. It had to move freely for wind changes and to stop the boat tipping, as well as for when they needed to collapse it.

***

It was now late afternoon and they had worked hard and were delighted with their work. Grinning from ear to ear, Jack and Tom congratulated each other. Their hopes were back up. They cheered and gave each other a high five.

"Let's check the fishing line and get a fire going again. I really enjoyed that fish last night." Jack was feeling good and ready for supper. "I've been thinking, what do you think about grinding up a few biscuits, mixing the crumbs with coconut flesh and baking it in a big leaf? I think it might work."

"Why not, anything to make those biscuits taste better will be a bonus." They walked together to check out the fishing line.

"Yes! Another fish, same kind too and even bigger!" Tom yelled out in delight.

"Fantastic! What about baiting the hook and seeing if we can get another tonight?" Jack was thinking ahead.

"You get the fire going then and I'll do just that."

Tom made his way to the box to where the salt pork was to cut a piece for bait and set up the fishing line, taking the fish with him to clean it and prepare it for cooking. Meanwhile, Jack climbed up above the beach to gather some firewood.

With the fish ready and the fire set, Jack got to work with his tinder box. He quickly got the kindling going then the smaller twigs. Soon the fire was going strongly.

Jack took a handful of hardtack biscuits and using a large round stone he had picked off the beach, ground them up in one of their coconut cups using a stubby stick, like a mortar and pestle. Chopping through one of the coconuts they had collected earlier, he poured the milk into the other coconut shell cup. Cutting down to the shell he broke it open and cut out the flesh. Chopping it up, he mixed it with the biscuit crumbs with a bit of coconut milk and formed a cake-like lump of pastry. To finish off he wrapped the fish and the biscuit mixture in some leaf parcels which he then placed in the hot coals.

Sitting on a box each, Jack and Tom gazed into the fire and waited for their supper to cook. There was a sense of anticipation between them that was nothing to do with food. It was about getting home. They had been away for nearly two weeks and their parents and family must be distraught.

Breaking the spell, Jack got a stick and dragged the parcels out of the fire. Opening the leaf parcels the steam rose from the fish and looked ready to slice up and eat. The coconut and biscuit mixture came out as a lightly browned pudding.

Tom cut up the fish just as he had the previous night. Sharing out the fish and biscuit confection onto their wooden keg tops, they tucked in.

"Hey Jack, that's not bad, tasty and goes well with the fish."

With his mouth full, he replied, "It's my natural talent, I can't help it. Think I'll become a TV chef when we get back."

"You'll need to improve your table manners, old chap. No one will want to look into your gob and see you chomping your signature dishes."

They both laughed. They were excited but worried at the same time. They had no idea if they would find Pigeon Island, let alone get through the cave and arrive home.

"Let's check the fishing line. I'll bring a one of those flaming branches to use as a torch." Tom stood up and got hold of the end of a branch resting on the ground, the other end flaming in the fire.

Walking the few yards to the fishing line they were amazed at their luck. Another catch. It seemed that the local fish liked salt pork.

"This is such a great place. In different circumstances I wouldn't mind a holiday here!" Jack enthused.

"Actually Jack, I hope I never see this place again. I want to go home and stay there. We're lucky that we're both practical guys and are able to tackle different problems that we're faced with."

"Yeah, you're right, although we have no choice. I'm sure we're going to make it. Come on, let's get the fish cooked and we'll get it wrapped up for the journey. We'll find more coconuts in the morning, load the boat with anything we think we need and get on with it."

After cleaning and cooking the fish in the remaining embers of the fire, they left it in its leaf package and put it in the box with the pork and hard tack biscuits. Tom retrieved the fishing line wound it around its frame and put it into one of the other boxes they had decided to load on the boat for the journey.

The night was darker than usual, there were no stars and a breeze had sprung up. Tom looked up and a large raindrop hit him in the eye. More drops followed rapidly. Tom leapt under the shelter. Jack followed close behind. The skies opened and the rain poured down and the noise on the canvas was deafening. It was so hard, it was bouncing off the sand into the shelter, which made the boys huddle close together under the middle.

"Let's hope this clears by tomorrow. I don't fancy setting off in rain. We might have to bail the boat, the wind might be too strong and visibility will be poor." Jack's emotions were up and down like a yo-yo.

"This is the tropics, Jack. We've been to Florida with a similar climate and our experience is that it never lasts that long."

"I know, but I can't remember it raining there at night, only during the day."

"Well, if we have to delay for a day, then that's the way it has to be. We should try to get some sleep."

"Yeah, you're right."

Ten

Jack stirred and opened his eyes. The rain had stopped and as he sat up, he could see the sky was clear but to the west, the rain clouds filled the horizon. Tom was still asleep, curled up on his right side. Looking up at the underside of the canvas it was bowed downwards. He climbed outside to find their shelter was holding quite a bit of rainwater. It had done its job though.

"Wakey, wakey, Tom. Time to go home. C'mon pal, let's get moving!"

Tom groaned and stretched. Craning his neck from under the canvas he almost yelled, "It's stopped raining, good! Let's collect a few coconuts for the journey then have some grub." He crawled out and looked around. The sea looks quite calm out beyond the reef. "A great day for going home!"

They set off along the beach. Apart from the first day, they really hadn't had time to look around the island as they had been working from dawn till dusk. It really was a beautiful place. After walking for a few hundred yards they had collected four coconuts each, which was all they could carry on a single trip. Two more trips, going a bit further each time and they had collected twelve in total. They took them straight to the boat.

Tom made an obvious observation, "There's a couple of inches of rain water in the bottom."

"It should be okay though." There would have to be a hole in the bottom to stop Jack now.

Tom was grinning, feeling confident of their escape. "I rather fancy some pork, hard tack biscuits all washed down with some coconut milk, followed by a little coconut flesh, for breakfast. How about you Jack?"

"Err… no. I'd like two fried eggs, bacon and toast please."

"I'm afraid they are off the menu today. I can only give you a slice of salt pork between two slices of hard tack biscuit with fresh coconut to follow, sir."

"Oh, err… ummm… alright then. Sounds wonderful." They both laughed at the silliness of their situation.

Tom sliced the pork while Jack chopped at a couple of coconuts. He poured the milk into their cups and chopped the outer husk down to the flesh filled inner shell. They ate quickly, without talking. Both of them lost in thought. Trepidation and hope. The atmosphere was electric.

In a hurry now to get started, they put two boxes of kit, spare ropes, axes, machetes and their meagre food rations on board. Taking the rum kegs to the stream they filled them with water and carried these between them to the boat. They secured the kegs to one of the seat boards near to the mast.

"I think we should take down the canvas off the shelter and take it with us. We may need it. We can at least cover the kegs in case a wave breaks over the boat and spoils the water." Tom said.

"Yeah, good idea let's do it and get this boat into the water."

It took the boys less time to take down their shelter than put it up. They folded the shelter and carried it to the boat where they spread it over the kegs. Looking around, they could see nothing else they needed or wanted. Hopefully, they had everything required for what should be a fairly short trip.

"Let's launch the boat then and get off." Tom's voice wobbled with emotion.

They stood behind the boat, still standing on the logs they had moved it on two days ago. The beach sloped slightly which should make their task easier. Moving behind it, they got ready to push.

Ready, Tom? On the count of three. ONE! TWO! THREE! Push!

Pushing with their shoulders against the back of the boat, it edged forward.

"It's moving Jack, quick, get round to the front with a log underneath!"

Tom pushed steadily while Jack ran to the back, picking up logs and moving them to the front. It was tough work but they were succeeding as ten minutes later, the bow was in the water and Jack ran to the back and they pushed harder. The boat ran off the last log and was in the water and floating.

"Yes!" They were ecstatic. They gave each other a high five and climbed into the boat. Jack grabbed the rope at the end of the boom and got the sail into wind. They moved at an angle to the beach, Tom took the rudder. They were soon away from the shore, cutting along in the fresh breeze. They headed for the the gap in the reef which was a good hundred yards wide. The waves in the gap were small and as they went through, the boat rose and fell slightly. Turning due west, using the compass on his digital watch, Jack moved to the starboard side of the boat and held the boom rope and the sail billowed. The boy's excitement was palpable.

The sun was climbing in the sky now. Jack knew that sailing off a compass was difficult because a few degrees off course over thirty miles would mean missing Pigeon Island by a good margin. Looking round, Santa Inez island was growing smaller behind them.

After a couple of hours, they were still moving along in the breeze in a westerly direction, the island now well out of sight. There was no turning back now. The sun blazed down and the boys drank from the kegs using their coconut shell cups. Their enthusiasm was waning. They knew that it would take most of a day or so to cover the thirty miles as long as the breeze held up but the frustration of not knowing how far they had sailed was intense.

When they had been going for three hours, they lunched on biscuits and coconut milk. The boys only spoke occasionally. It seemed neither wanted to expose their worries to the other. The afternoon drew on.

"What speed do you think we're doing here Jack?"

"Three knots or so?"

"How long have we been going?"

"Almost four hours."

"Hmm… about six hours to go at this speed then." Tom sounded doubtful.

***

After eight hours there was no sign of land as darkness fell, but they couldn't allow themselves to fall asleep, as tired as they were. Tom tied the rudder so he could get the food out.

Spending a bit of time cutting up the fish, sharing only part of it out with some biscuits, he said, "We should ration our food, err, just in case we umm… lose the wind and it takes us a bit longer." He didn't want to admit that they might get lost and would need as much food as they could get. He took the boom rope while Jack ate and then they swapped over. The boys finished up with a cup of water each. They had been travelling all day and were prepared to stay awake and keep going as long as necessary.

It was a long night and no dark silhouette of land appeared for them. Their eyes burned with need for sleep and from staring out into the darkness, searching the darkness for land. They both felt like crying. The night came and went and after what seemed an age, the first signs of light appeared behind them in the east.

Dawn broke and when light enough, they searched all horizons for land but there was nothing in sight. The boys looked at each other and Jack gave a crooked smile.

Downhearted but not beaten, Jack said, "Come on Tom, we should cheer up and be positive. We've no idea what speed we've been making overnight, Pigeon Island could be just over the horizon."

"It might be, but I'm slightly worried about the look of those clouds behind us. I've been keeping an eye on them and they are getting closer. It could be a rain storm. Rain storms are almost always accompanied by wind."

Jack looked beyond Tom at the cloud formation building up and it was getting bigger. "We'll collapse the sail by tying it to the mast with the boom rope if we get a strong wind, we can't afford to be capsized or have the mast blown over."

Tom's fears were proved right. The wind stiffened and they were cutting along at a faster rate. The clouds were catching up and they could see the rain underneath them. As the sky darkened and rain began to fall on them as they couldn't actually drop the sail because it was securely tied above head height, Jack folded the sail up to the mast by turning the boom ninety degrees and then using a length of rope, bound it to the mast. The rain was now falling heavily, they were wet through in moments. Wind was whipping up the waves and the boat was now tossing around. The speed of arrival and the ferocity of the storm was shocking.

Unfolding the piece of canvas which had been their shelter they pulled it over their heads to keep the rain off, making sure that they kept the water kegs covered. This was terrible, if they had been on course before the storm they were now thrown completely at the mercy of the sea and goodness knows where they would end up, if anywhere at all.

The storm lasted about two hours, and when the rain stopped, they had to do some bailing out with their shell cups. The cloud travelled on westwards, the sky cleared and the sun was climbing in the sky. Untying the sail Jack took control of the boom and off they sailed westerly again, but they had even less idea if they were sailing towards Pigeon Island than they had before.

It occurred to Tom that they hadn't eaten for ages and suggested a couple of biscuits and some water. Jack agreed, not really hungry but he certainly had a burning feeling in his belly. The biscuits seemed drier than usual and they both had to wash them down with extra water.

The day wore on, the heat and humidity relentless.

"We're lost, Tom. We've been heading west for one and a half days now and nothing in sight. We must have been blown off course by the storm." Jack's face was solemn.

Tom tried to smile to lighten the atmosphere as he replied, "Yes, I reckon we are but the good news is that if we can last out with our food and water, we'll eventually hit some land, if not another island, we will certainly hit Mexico or central America and civilisation, whatever that is in this century. We should reduce the amount we're eating and drinking, just in case we need to make supplies last."

The afternoon turned to evening and on agreement that on the basis they had no idea where they were, they had nothing to lose by tying the tiller and boom in position and get some rest. They were exhausted from lack of sleep, only adrenalin had kept them going. Hopefully, the boat would continue westwards, pushed along by the steady breeze. They pulled the canvas up onto the sides of the boat to act as a shelter. Underneath and huddled in the bottom of the boat, the boys fell almost immediately into a deep sleep.

Night fell and as it did, the wind changed direction and the boat with it. Unknown to the sleeping boys, they were now headed north west.

***

It was breaking light when Jack awoke. His muscles were stiff and sore from the hard floor of the boat and not least, sleeping in about an inch of water. He checked his watch compass and was devastated to find that they had been travelling in the wrong direction, perhaps all night.

"Aaagghh!" Jack cried out loudly.

Tom woke and said, "I was just dreaming of being at home until you shattered my illusion with your foghorn voice. What's going on, can you see anything?"

"Well, dreaming might be as close as you get to home, we've been sailing the wrong way all night. We'll change course when I've had a pee."

Tom groaned, "How much more of this can we take. Can nothing go right?"

Jack was standing, peeing over the side of the boat when he cried out, "What's that over there Tom?" Jack pointed to the the north east. He couldn't believe his eyes, perhaps it was a mirage but he had spotted something a few miles away.

Tom stood up, "Look, it's a ship!" He was stunned.

"Oh no," groaned Jack. "Please, no more Pirates!"

"They're heading this way I think! What shall we do?"

"Damned if I know, how can we outrun a ship? Let's keep going, they may not have seen us and their direction is just a coincidence." Wishful thinking from Jack.

They could make out the ship in silhouette as it made headway. They could make out a large triangular sail.

"It's a sloop, so it's probably not pirates," Tom heaved a sigh of relief.

"Yes, I can make it out now. Maybe they'll help us." Jack sounded hopeful.

"Unless it's more Spaniards who want to take us home to Cornwall!"

"What? How could they know unless it's El Conde or his men?"

"I'm just tossing out possibilities, it may just be innocent traders who've spotted us and are coming to check us out."

The sloop was making good speed, after a half hour or so it was only several hundred yards away from the boys. Someone was standing on the bow with a telescope. They watched him drop the telescope in one hand to his side and he began waving and shouting.

"It's Jasper! It's the Sussex Oak, it didn't sink!" Jack was ecstatic.

Waving furiously the boys were so pleased they were leaping up and down with the boat rocking from side to side so much they nearly fell overboard.

"Get that sail tied up Jack so they can come alongside."

Jack did as he had done during the storm, by folding the sail upwards he tied the boom to the mast. Their boat stopped and was rocking gently as the sloop pulled expertly alongside. One of the crew dropped two ropes, one of which Tom tied to the bow, the other Jack tied to the stern, they were pulled in against the side of the ship. A rope ladder was thrown over the side for the boys to climb up and as they did, Jasper was looking down at them with a beaming smile.

"I cannot believe my eyes! I thought you two were dead, washed overboard and drowned."

Jumping over the ships' rail, the boys hugged Jasper. Tom explained, "We thought you had sunk in the storm, we got washed ashore on Santa Inez Island along with the rowing boat and a few supplies."

Captain Holbrook appeared and was obviously very pleased to see Jack and Tom too.

"Good to see you lads alive and well. And thank you for bringing my rowing boat back! You did well to get this far, we're only ten nautical miles from Pigeon Island. If we hadn't seen you first, I reckon the course you were on would have taken you straight there!"

Jack and Tom looked at each other and began to laugh almost hysterically. They were almost home!

"Come on, we'll go straight to the galley and get you some food." Jasper put his arms around their shoulders and walked the boys to the stairs which led below deck.

Seated in the Sir James' cabin they were served fried eggs with rather hard bread but it was a wonderful change from what they had been eating the past few days.

"What happened to you chaps in the storm after we err… got off before we should?"

Jack was speaking with his mouth full again. "Did you lose a sail, because we found one which is how we managed to rig a piece of it for the boat and as a shelter."

Jasper politely finished his mouthful of food and cleared his voice. "No we lost a spare sail that was tied up on deck, which must be the one you found. We were driven by the wind for many a mile, we took on a great amount of water but miraculously stayed afloat. The Captain did a marvellous job of running with the wind while we rode out the storm. We ended up in Grand Cayman where we spent a day repairing damage, pumping out the water we had taken on and set sail to look for you two. We saw a small sailing boat but never dreamt it might be you. You must tell me how you managed to survive and how you got to here."

Tom, pushing his empty plate to one side, told their story with Jack adding in bits that he thought Tom had missed. At the end, Jasper was very impressed.

"What an amazing story, gentlemen. You should write an account of your adventures, Kate and my father will be in awe of your tenacity."

Jack replied, "We just want to get home, Jasper. We were determined to achieve that and would do anything to get there."

"Of course, that's understandable. Come on, let's go to the deck and we can look out for Pigeon Island, your route home."

Eleven

A speck of land appeared on the western horizon. Jack and Tom were grinning like Cheshire cats. Hopefully, their skiff was where they had left it two weeks ago. The landmass got bigger and they could make out the ragged treeline and beaches.

"Look Jack, I can see the Cave! The beach where we were caught is over to the left."

"Yes! There's our skiff, it's up the beach a little but it's there alright!"

Excitement was high as they got closer to the island. Two hundred yards offshore, the Captain had the sloop heave-to and drop anchor. Approaching the boys he addressed them.

"Right my young gentlemen. I'd be delighted to get you ashore now. Is that your little boat I can see on the beach yonder?"

"Yes it is, and yes please, we would be delighted to be rowed ashore." Tom's voice almost squeaked, such was his excitement.

Captain Holbrook ordered a boat to be lowered. It wasn't the one the boys had used to effect there escape from Santa Inez, there was a bit of work to be done to bring that one back to its normal state. The rowing crew clambered down the side and waited for Jack and Tom.

The Captain shook hands with the boys and grinning, said, "Well, I wish you lads the very best of luck and hope that your little adventure hasn't put you off sailing."

"Well maybe for a while, Captain," Jack responded. "Thank you very much for everything and especially for finding us and bringing us here."

Tom echoed that sentiment but couldn't wait to get over the side and into the rowing boat.

"Go on then, get off with you… and don't come back." The Captain had a wry sense of humour and was grinning ear to ear as he spoke.

Jasper got into the boat with the boys, wanting to see them off and on their way home. He was pleased for them but sad at the same time. They had gone through a lot together and had developed a sort of brotherly affection for each other.

Once seated in the boat, one of the oarsmen pushed away from the sloop with an oar, took his seat and on command from the sailor at the tiller, all eight men started rowing towards the beach. The last time Jack and Tom had travelled in this direction was when they were being chased by the pirates. The boat crew aimed for the skiff using strong powerful strokes, propelling the boat across the water very quickly. The distance from the sloop to the beach was covered in minutes. As they approached the shore, on command the rowers shipped their oars and the boat glided into the soft sand at the water's edge.

The crew leapt out and pushed the boat further up onto the beach. Jack and Tom waded ashore after getting out and walked to their skiff. It was exactly as they had left it, although fortunately it had been washed by waves slightly higher up the beach, rather than the alternative which might have been where it was pulled out to sea. The oars were tucked inside and their life jackets lay in a bit of water in the bottom.

With the help of a couple of sailors, they dragged the skiff into the water. Standing at the water's edge, they said their goodbyes to Jasper, whom they had first met, when hiding in a cave further inland on the island when he found them but didn't give them away. Jasper who had patiently shown them the duties of a Powder Boy. He had befriended them and eventually rescued them from possible death. They would miss him and his friendship.

"Goodbye my friends, I still don't understand where you come from or where you are going back to but I hope we will meet again some day." Jasper looked and sounded sad.

"It's been a pleasure knowing you, Jasper," said Jack. And thank you for everything. Without your help we wouldn't be here." Jack felt a tear well in his eye as he spoke.

"Jasper, you have been a true and brave friend. We are going to miss you. Thanks for everything." Tom was emotional and had never said anything like that to anyone before.

The boys climbed in the boat and donned their life jackets and waving goodbyes, then started to row along the cliff edge towards the cave. The crew pushed their boat back into deeper water, got in and rowed up just behind the skiff, following them. Jack and Tom, rowing with an oar each glanced over their shoulders to check direction and approaching quickly was the mouth of the cave that they had come through, although only two weeks ago, seemed like a lifetime. Suddenly, they felt the pull of the current taking them into the cave, just as it had done on the other side when their adventure had begun.

Yelling their goodbyes to Jasper, they were pulled into the cave and lost sight of the rowing boat. Their excitement rose a few notches.

"Well, this is it Tom, we're on our way home," Jack was almost delirious.

"I'm as happy and optimistic as you Jack, but I just hope we don't pop out of this crazy cave at the time of the dinosaurs or a World War Two battle or something."

"Oh trust you to wreck my homecoming! I hadn't even thought of that."

The luminosity of the water and the warm, humid air lessened, it got darker and there was no light from the cave mouth now. A few moments later it was pitch dark. The skiff was still moving but they could see nothing. It was eerie, they could hear their own hearts beating.

"Look Jack, daylight!"

A dim light was opening up in front of them and getting lighter every minute. They could hear waves somewhere ahead. Soon they could see full daylight and they held their breaths quite spontaneously, waiting to see where they were. The current propelled them into open water.

"Yes! We're home!" Jack almost screamed it out.

It was Mennan Cove.

"Yes but what year is it?" Tom was doing his pessimist thing.

"Oh, shut up! Those cars up on the harbour wall look like the ones we left behind two weeks ago. Let's get rowing ashore."

Sitting side by side, Jack and Tom, hearts racing, excitement building, made short work of the distance to the harbour wall steps. Shipping the oars, they tied the skiff to a ring embedded in the wall. With their legs trembling slightly they climbed the steps and stood looking around them.

"There's Mr Goodwin the fishmonger in his van over there. He doesn't look any younger or older, so we must be back in our own time era," Jack said.

Tom grinning, replied, "It could be his son Jimmy, twenty years on."

"Idiot!"

They began to run, heading for home. Ten minutes later they entered the road Jack lived in and they saw that Tom's mother's car was outside the Andrew's house. They slowed, catching their breath. Jack looked at his watch, it was ten past four.

"They are probably having a cup of tea together and supporting each other about the loss of their sons. They truly must think we're dead."

Rushing around to the back door, the boys crashed in to the kitchen where both mothers were sitting and were indeed drinking tea, eating scones and jam.

The boys stared with puzzled looks at their mums, astounded that they hardly seemed bothered.

Jack's mum put down her cup and said, "Hello boys. Have you had a good day?"

About the Author

I am Trevor Anderson, father and grandfather, retired and living in the South-East of England.

Since childhood, I have always been and still am, an avid reader. I'm passionate about literacy and love the way books open minds; and how even a fictional story with some historical basis, can lead to a learning opportunity through curiosity and discovery of the actual background. This passion led me to the decision some time ago, that I would write a book for children, with the kind of story that I would have enjoyed as a child, packed with adventure, danger and thrills; and a basis in history. I believe I have achieved that with this book.

"The Time Cave – Spanish Main" is set mainly in the early 1700s, during the "Golden Age of Piracy".

Available worldwide from Amazon

Michael Terence
Publishing

www.mtp.agency

mtp.agency

@mtp_agency

Milton Keynes UK
Ingram Content Group UK Ltd.
UKHW011041080324
439029UK00001B/67

9 781800 947269